**Look for other titles about the
WILD AT HEART vet volunteers:**

✿✿✿✿✿
Missing Cat!!
✿✿✿✿✿

Socrates

Huge orange male tabby. May be injured!!

 **Please call!!!**

Wild at Heart Veterinary Clinic at **555-WILD**

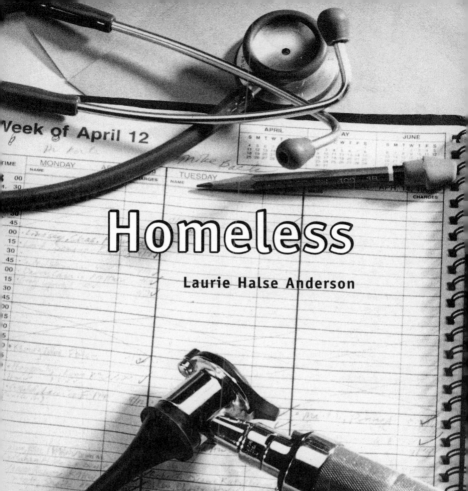

Homeless

Laurie Halse Anderson

SCHOLASTIC INC.

New York   Toronto   London   Auckland   Sydney
Mexico City   New Delhi   Hong Kong   Buenos Aires

American Girl®

Acknowledgments

Thanks to Kimberly Michels, D.V.M., and Judith Tamas, D.V.M., for their consultation and review of veterinary procedures and practices.

ISBN 0-439-39220-9

12 11 10 9 8 7 6 5 4 3 2 1   2 3 4 5 6 7/0

Printed in the U.S.A.   40

First Scholastic printing, March 2002

Series Editor: Julie Williams
Art Direction: Jane Varda
Design: Joshua Mjaanes
Photography: Mark Salisbury, Jamie Young
Veterinary Consultant: Kimberly Michels, D.V.M.

Photo Credits: page 127—Index Stock/Fotopic; page 128—CORBIS/Yann Arthus; page 129—Index Stock/Omni Photo Communications, Inc.; page 130—Photodisc/Russell Illig

Dedication

To Sarah and Liz Morrison. May you always be wild at heart!

ONE

I still think you need a cat, Sunita," Zoe tells me as we bounce along in the school bus. We're going to Wild at Heart, the veterinary clinic where we volunteer. It's the perfect way to start the weekend.

"Forget about it," I say. "It's useless. My mother won't let me. End of story."

"You're giving up too easily." Zoe fixes the butterfly clips in her hair. "You like cats more than anyone I know."

She has a point. I've always loved cats. Long-haired, short-haired, tabby, Siamese, or stray. I adore them all. I can watch cats for hours—the graceful way they move, that mysterious look in their eyes, the twitching tail, the cute whiskers—everything about them fascinates me.

My mother, however, doesn't like them. I think they scare her, though she won't admit it. Instead, she gives reasons like "They shed" or "They'll ruin the furniture with their claws." She has made up her mind. No cats in the Patel house.

"You just haven't asked the right way," Zoe continues. "Parents expect you to ask a million times so they know you really, really, really want something. You've probably only asked, like, a thousand times."

Zoe's mother is an actress. I'm sure she doesn't mind if Zoe gets a little dramatic when she wants something. That doesn't work at my house.

"My mother isn't the kind of person who likes being asked a million times for anything," I explain. "She's a doctor. She wants facts."

Zoe's redheaded cousin, Maggie MacKenzie, leans across the aisle. "The fact is you're great with cats and you deserve a pet," she says.

David Hutchinson turns around in the seat in front of us. "Tell your mom that a cat would eat the mice in your basement," he says.

"Yuck!" Zoe protests. "That's disgusting."

Brenna Lake, sitting next to David, punches his arm lightly. "Sunita doesn't have mice, you bean head." She twists around to face Zoe and me. "Write down all the reasons why you want a cat and give the list to your mom. Make sure you have lots."

"I doubt that would work," I say with a laugh. "My mother wants a cat that doesn't have fur, claws, or teeth, or need a litter box or food. In other words, she'll let me have a stuffed animal."

"But she let you volunteer at the clinic," Maggie says. "Remember how much that surprised you? Maybe you should give her a chance."

She's right about that. I didn't expect Mother to let me volunteer with the others. But she did. At first I thought helping at the clinic would be enough. If I got to be around cats at Wild at Heart, I wouldn't want one of my own so badly. But being around them makes me want one of my own even more. There has to be something I can do to get Mother to change her mind.

The bus slows as we approach our stop.

"OK, you guys," I say, turning to my friends. "You've convinced me. I'll try asking my mother again. But I have to find the right way to do it. Now let's get to Wild at Heart."

Wild at Heart Animal Clinic is run by Dr. J.J. MacKenzie, Maggie and Zoe's grandmother. We call her Dr. Mac. She invited Brenna, David, and me to volunteer at the clinic with Maggie and Zoe last month, and it's the most spectacular thing that has ever happened to me.

Being at the clinic is amazing. We see all kinds of animals, from cats to canaries, puppies to potbellied pigs. My favorite parts are when the veterinarians let us help them during examinations and when we learn about things like X rays and blood tests.

It's not always fun, though. Some of the work is boring and smelly, like cleaning cages or mopping floors. But every job is important—that's what Dr. Mac says.

Since my dream is to be a vet when I grow up, I'll do whatever she asks. I want to know everything I can about animals. Especially cats. Whenever I have any free time at home, I devour the cat books that Dr. Mac lets me borrow, or surf the Internet to find Web sites about cats.

All this reading may explain why Socrates likes me. Socrates is huge. Twenty pounds of muscle and attitude. His fur is a blend of orange, rust, and yellow that reminds me of apricots. You can see faint stripes on his tail. I bet he had a tabby cat for a grandfather.

Socrates has the reputation of being an aloof, "worship but don't touch me" cat. Maggie says that he rarely lets her pet him or pick him up. He likes to sleep on Dr. Mac's desk or on the receptionist's counter, but he takes off if anyone tries to scratch under his chin or between his ears.

That's why Maggie and Dr. Mac were so surprised when Socrates hopped into my lap a few weeks ago. He had never done that to anyone else before. It's like he picked me to be his favorite human. He always walks up to me when I enter the clinic and lets me pet him for a few minutes. If I sit down, he sits with me. Maggie thinks he likes the smell of my shampoo. (I have long black hair, and he does like to play with it.) Dr. Mac says he cuddles with me because I'm a calm and quiet person.

I have a different idea. Socrates knows how much I want a cat of my own. He can tell that I love him. I think he's adopted me. I guess I've adopted him, too. I've adopted him in my heart. He's like my pet away from home—until I get my own.

We round the corner, and Wild at Heart comes into sight. Dr. Mac's house is a two-story brick building with dark green shutters and a matching green door. The clinic pokes out of the left side of the house, a one-story addition. It has its own door and two windows that face the street. A garden of spring flowers blooms along the entire front of the building. Dr. Mac says that animals enjoy flowers just as much as people do.

Socrates shoulders his way out of the daffodils to greet me as we get closer. He butts his head against my shins, and I crouch down to pet him.

"Hello, Socrates!" I say.

He purrs loudly, like a lawn mower engine, and rubs the corner of his mouth against my knuckles. Cats have special scent glands on their faces, and when they rub against a person like this, it's a way of marking their territory. It's kind of nice that Socrates thinks I'm part of his world.

"You should feel how warm his fur is," I tell the others as I lay my hand on his back. "I bet he's been lying in the sun all afternoon."

"Cats have all the fun," David says. "Eat, sleep. Eat, sleep, sleep, sleep. Eat some more. Wish I could do that."

"Hey, look!" Zoe says, pointing to the corner of the yard. "Another cat. Do you think Socrates has a girlfriend?"

The new cat steps delicately onto the grass and walks toward us. It's a tuxedo cat, mostly black with white paws and a patch of white on her chest. It's easy to see this is a she-cat. She's very pregnant, with a heavy belly that almost touches the ground.

Socrates stiffens and growls. I can feel the vibration of his warning call under my fingertips. He doesn't want her here, and he's telling her she should leave.

"Shh," I say quietly. "She's not going to hurt you. Just relax and be friendly."

Socrates is not in the mood to be nice. He steps away from me to face the black cat, his ears flat against his head. His tail whips back and forth, warning the other cat.

"*Hisssss!*"

It looks like fur is going to fly.

TWO

Why is he doing this?" I ask Maggie. "He doesn't mind it when cats come into the clinic."

"Socrates knows it's OK for other cats to come into the clinic, but the yard is his alone," Maggie says calmly. "Don't worry. She'll run off in a second. That's what always happens. I wonder where she belongs, though. I've never seen her around here."

"Maybe she's looking for a place to make her nest," I say. "It looks like she'll be ready to have her kittens soon. Let's get Socrates inside and leave her alone."

The black cat takes two more steps toward Socrates. She makes a strange warbling noise in her throat and arches her back, her fur standing on end. Cats do that so they look bigger, to frighten away other animals.

Socrates is not scared. His coat is all puffed up

too, making him look monstrously huge. He opens his mouth wide to show his sharp teeth and lets out another loud hiss.

Maggie frowns. "That's not good," she says.

"Duh!" Brenna says.

"Maybe—" I start, but before I can finish the sentence, the cats jump on each other. Socrates lashes out with his claws, then chases the female behind the azalea bushes. The bushes shake as the cats growl, hiss, and howl in pain.

"We have to do something!" I cry.

"What?" asks David.

"I'll get the hose!" Maggie says as she runs for the side of the house. "Water always stops a cat fight."

The tuxedo cat bolts out of the bushes, with Socrates hot on her heels. She stops at the corner of the building and turns her claws on him. He pounces. They go at it again. Someone is going to get hurt!

"Hurry, Maggie!" Zoe calls.

I take a step toward the fighting cats.

"No, Sunita!" Brenna shouts as she grabs my shirt and pulls me back. "Don't touch them. You'll get hurt. He's furious—if you try to stop him, he might bite or scratch you."

She's right. I've never seen Socrates like this before.

The two cats separate and try to stare each other down. I gasp at the sight of blood dripping from a bite on Socrates' cheek. There's a gash on his hind leg, too. The tuxedo cat won't put her front right paw on the ground, and I can see where Socrates bit her shoulder. She turns sideways and Socrates prepares to pounce again.

"Stand back!" Maggie calls as she returns, dragging the hose behind her.

She presses the handle of the nozzle and sprays the angry cats. Both of them take off down the street like they were shot out of a cannon.

"Socrates!" I shout. "Come back!"

Socrates and the tuxedo cat disappear around the corner.

"We've got to follow them," I say urgently. "They're both bleeding."

"I'll come with you," Maggie says, dropping the hose on the ground.

"Me too!" Brenna and David say together.

"I'll stay and tell Gran what happened," Zoe says. "Hurry, you guys!"

We run after the cats—first down the block, then around the corner and through a long alley. Maggie sprints ahead of the rest of us.

"I can see them," she shouts. "This way."

We race down another alley, then come out by the gas station at the intersection of Roosevelt Avenue and Dorset Street. Two cars are getting gassed up at the station, but there is no sign of any cats.

"Are you sure they came this way?" Brenna asks, scanning the block.

"Positive," Maggie answers.

"Maybe they turned somewhere," David suggests.

"You kids looking for something?" asks a man pumping gas.

"A cat," Brenna answers. "Actually, two of them, one orange and one black. Have you seen them?"

"Just a minute ago," the man says. "They ran across the street."

I look at the others. "Let's go."

Directly across from the gas station is an old button factory, abandoned and locked up tight.

"Socrates couldn't get inside," Maggie points out as she scans the front of the building. "I bet he turned around and went home another way."

"I don't think so," I say. "I think he's here."

"Why?" David asks.

"I don't know," I answer, looking up and down the street for a sign of Socrates. "A hunch maybe, a feeling. Maybe he chased her back here. Let's check around the back of the building."

Behind the factory is a loading area totally overgrown with trees, bushes, and weeds. I bet this would look like heaven to a cat on the run.

"You guys, come look!" I shout.

They jog over.

"You could hide a hundred cats back here," I say. "Socrates is in there, I'm sure of it. We need to look for him."

"How are we supposed to get through all the bushes?" Brenna asks.

"I don't know, Sunita," Maggie says. "Even if he is in there, we'll never find him."

"Let's see how far we can go," I say, stepping into the weeds and pushing some branches out of my way. "Socrates! Here, kitty, kitty!"

"Hey, Soc! Here, Soc," Maggie calls.

It's slow going. We have to stay bent over because of the heavy vines and branches that pull at our hair and clothes. There better not be poison ivy in here.

"This place is a maze. We should leave a trail of gingerbread crumbs like Hansel and Gretel,"

Brenna grumbles. "Remember, you guys are coming to my house for dinner tonight. My parents will flip out if we're late."

I almost trip over something on the ground. It looks like a piece of rusted machinery.

"Watch your step," I warn. "Here, Socrates!"

"This is so cool!" David exclaims behind me. "It's like a jungle back here. Makes me want to do my Tarzan yell."

"Don't!" we all say at the same time.

"OK, OK," he says. "You guys are no fun. Wait— did you see that?"

A slim black tail slips through the wall of green a few steps ahead of us.

"It's the tuxedo cat!" I cry. "Socrates must be close by. Follow that cat!"

We push through the undergrowth faster.

"Where did she go?" Brenna asks.

"I don't know," David answers. "She disappeared again. Wait a minute…what's that?"

Up ahead, I see a broken-down, weathered red boxcar on rusted wheels.

"C'mon, the cats could be inside it," I say.

We edge around the high bushes surrounding the boxcar. I stop. Ten feet of broken concrete stretches from the boxcar to the railroad tracks, and the clearing is covered with cats!

"Oh, my gosh!" Brenna whispers.

"Awesome," Maggie declares.

"I don't believe it," David says quietly.

Neither do I. We crouch down in the weeds at the edge of the clearing. There must be thirty of them, chasing each other, sharpening their claws on the tree trunks, sunbathing, sleeping in overturned rusty barrels, scratching at fleas, and tiptoeing around broken glass. A few look sleek and power-ful, but most are thin, flea-bitten, and in need of a good brushing.

A black-and-white kitten is batting at a beetle. A dirty white cat with blue eyes is trying to clean its tail. A gray cat with a crooked tail hops out of the open door of the boxcar, then pauses to lick its shoulder. There is no sign of Socrates or the black cat he was chasing.

"What is this place?" Brenna asks.

"Cat Land!" David says dramatically, gesturing with his arm toward the boxcar.

He's right. Someone has written CAT LAND on the boxcar door.

"I don't know who wrote that," Maggie says, "but if you ask me, we're looking at a colony of stray cats."

As I slowly step out of the weeds, the cats turn their heads to look at me. A few of them at the edges of the clearing vanish into the underbrush. The rest of them ignore me and go back to what they were doing, except for two cats with black-and-white patches who bound toward me.

"Meeeroww!" they call loudly.

"Sounds like they're hungry," Maggie says.

"I wish I had some treats to give them," I say, crouching down to pet the friendly cats. They tilt their heads back as I scratch under their chins. "You sure are sweet," I murmur. "How did you get here? Where are your owners?"

"I don't think they have any," Brenna says.

I look at my friends. This is no place for cats to live. Cats need a warm house, with people who have warm laps. They need food, clean water, a litter box, and a scratching post they can shred to bits. A windowsill so they can watch the world passing outside. Most of all, cats need friendly owners who will pet them and groom them and make a fuss.

The cats here have nothing. I wish I could take them all home.

"We have to do something," I say. "Tell Dr. Mac, or Captain Thompson at the shelter. We have to find Socrates, too."

Suddenly, a loud horn sounds, startling us and sending the rest of the cats dashing into the tall weeds. The train to Philadelphia roars down the tracks toward us.

It's so loud I can barely hear myself think. Brenna is trying to say something, but I can't hear her. She stands there moving her mouth and gesturing with her hands while the train rushes by, sending dry leaves and dust swirling through the air.

"What?" I shout.

The last train car whooshes by, and it's quiet again.

"Someone is coming," Brenna repeats, pointing.

On the other side of the tracks is a block of small houses, each with a tiny yard surrounded by a low fence. A boy wearing a green backpack cautiously walks across one of the yards toward us. He's followed by a little girl carefully carrying a plastic bowl that has water sloshing over the side. The boy looks like a third-grader. The girl is younger, first grade maybe, or kindergarten.

They unlatch the fence gate, walk through the opening, and latch it behind them. The boy pauses and carefully checks the tracks in both directions, then nods to the girl. They cross.

As they step into the clearing, the cats reappear

like magic, pouring out of the weeds, the trees, and the boxcar to greet them, meowing loudly. Some even walk up boldly to the newcomers and rub against their ankles. These kids are regulars.

"Hi," I say as I walk toward them. "Looks like your friends are happy to see you."

The little girl's eyes grow wide. The boy glares at me. I must have startled them.

"Who are you? What are you doing here?" he demands.

THREE

We're looking for a lost cat named Socrates," I say. "He's big, kind of an orange color, and he has a little cut on his face and a big one on his leg. He was in a fight. Last time we saw him, he was chasing a black female with white paws and a big belly—a tuxedo cat. We really need to find him. He's hurt."

I stop as my stomach tightens. I'm afraid for Socrates. What if we can't find him?

"He's from the vet clinic," David explains. "You know—Wild at Heart? We all work there."

"You aren't going to take the cats away?" the boy asks, his voice a little calmer now.

"No," Brenna says. "We just want to find Socrates and go home."

The boy walks over to the boxcar, keeping his eyes on us. He reaches in the open doorway and pulls two chipped ceramic bowls to the edge. Still watching us, he takes a small bag of cat food out of his backpack and empties it into the bowls. At the sound of food hitting the bowls, the cats run and leap into the boxcar to eat their meal.

The boy strokes the gray cat with the crooked tail. It looks like he is trying to make up his mind about something. He starts to speak, then stops. The little girl sets the water bowl on the ground and pets the cats that collect around it for a drink.

"The cats really like you," I say.

He nods.

"My name's Sunita," I say. "If you like cats, then you understand why we're worried. Socrates needs the veterinarian to look at his wounds. Can you help us find him?"

The boy hesitates for a moment. Then he looks me in the eye.

"All right. I'll look for him. But if he's back there"—he gestures toward the thick bushes that surround the clearing—"you'll never find him, trust me. My name's Jamie. Jamie Frazier." He pauses to slap a flea on his arm. "Do you know how to take care of a cat that's hurt?"

"Yes," I say. "A little. Do you have a hurt cat?"

Jamie looks at the girl, as if he's asking her permission for something. She nods her head slowly.

"Follow me," he says. "I got to show you something."

He leads us to an injured cat lying on a doll's blanket behind one of the rusted barrels. The cat's hind leg is swollen, and there's blood on the fur.

"I saw him get hit by a car yesterday," Jamie explains.

He pauses for a minute, like he's seeing the accident again. It must have been awful.

"He won't eat or drink anything. Don't get too close!" he warns as I stretch out my hand to feel for the cat's pulse. "He's one of the wild cats. You can't touch them, ever. They bite and scratch. The car knocked him out. I couldn't have touched him if he was awake."

"We have to get him to the clinic," I say.

"I'll call Gran," Maggie says, getting to her feet. "My grandmother is the vet. She needs to come and get him. We can't carry him back to the clinic, not in that shape."

"You can use the phone in our house. Katie will take you."

Katie takes Maggie's hand.

"Back in a second," Maggie calls as she and Katie cross the tracks and head for the Fraziers' house.

"I don't get it," Brenna says. "Are these all your cats? What's going on here?"

Jamie stands up and pulls his shoulders back with pride. "They aren't really ours, but we take care of them," he says.

"You feed them?" I ask.

Jamie nods. "We use our allowance money. Our parents won't let us take them into the house, so we play with them out here. The tame ones, that is. The wild cats bite."

"Look, Sunita," Brenna interrupts. "We have to keep looking for Socrates. David and I will start knocking on doors to see if any of the neighbors have seen him. We'll meet you back here in fifteen minutes."

"Good idea," I reply.

As they leave, Jamie asks me to describe the tuxedo cat again.

"I've seen her. She's around here all the time," he says. "We call her Mittens."

Before I can ask any more questions about Mittens, Maggie and Katie return, led by a short, angry woman wearing a smiley face T-shirt. The cats in the clearing scatter again, as they did when the train came through.

"Jamie Frazier, I told you to stay away from these

cats," the woman scolds. "And to keep your sister away from them, too. You know how dangerous they are."

As she gets closer, I can see that she's not angry, she's afraid. She stops in front of us and stares at the injured cat as if it were a snake about to bite her. The look on her face kind of reminds me of my mother.

"Is Dr. Mac coming, Maggie?" I ask.

"Gran said she'd be here soon." Maggie pauses, then speaks slowly and opens her eyes wide, like she's trying to send me a message. "This is Mrs. Frazier, Jamie and Katie's mother. Mrs. Frazier, this is my friend Sunita."

"Pleasure to meet you, Mrs. Frazier," I say politely. "You have nice kids. They really care about animals."

Mrs. Frazier doesn't smile the way most mothers do when you compliment their children. Instead, she turns to her son. "Take Katie into the house, Jamie. We'll talk about this later."

The brother and sister head for their house with sad faces. I don't understand any of this.

"They were just trying to help this cat." I point to the cat, still panting on the baby blanket. "It was hit by a car. We need to take it to the vet."

Mrs. Frazier waits until her kids have walked far

22

enough away that they won't hear her.

"I'm the head of the Chestnut Ridge Community Association," she explains. "I started getting calls about these cats a few months ago. The people in the neighborhood are upset. They say the cats are using their gardens for a bathroom and digging in their garbage."

She glances at the injured cat.

"There was an old man who used to live a few houses down from me. He'd leave out food for the cats. Well, he sold his house and moved, but the cats stayed around. At first I thought they were real cute, like you do."

She shakes her head. "Let me tell you something. One cat is cute. Two cats are fun. But you get a whole jungle of cats living in your backyard howling all night, and all of a sudden, it's trouble."

"Did you call the animal shelter?" Maggie asks.

"I tried calling everybody," Mrs. Frazier says, throwing her hands in the air. "I called the mayor, the city council, the county commissioners. With all the work they have to do, it takes a lot more than a few cats to get their attention. Meanwhile, these cats keep having kittens. Used to be a dozen or so back here, and now there have to be more than forty, maybe fifty."

"We could help you find homes for them," I say. "Get them adopted."

Mrs. Frazier smiles sympathetically. "Nobody is going to want these cats, honey, I promise you. They're wild. They're not pets. They bite, they scratch, and they have fleas. They're as bad as the raccoons that live back here. I bet they all have rabies and heaven knows what other diseases. That's why I want them out of here."

Her face softens for a minute. "I know my kids like them, but they're not safe. And we can't get a cat of our own, not with these mangy critters living at our back door." She sighs.

"We still have to take care of this one," I say. I crouch down to check on him. He's panting faster. I hope Dr. Mac gets here soon.

"You're foolish if you do," she says. "The county is coming tomorrow to take them away. All those months of phone calls have finally paid off."

The county is going to take them away?

"What are they going to do with them?" I ask.

Jamie steps out onto the back porch of his house. "Mom!" he calls. "Telephone!"

"I have to go," Mrs. Frazier says.

She walks away, then looks back at us over her shoulder. "I'm sorry you've lost your cat. I'll keep an eye out for him. But you better find him soon. Animal Control promised they'd be here first thing in the morning."

FOUR

Where's our patient?" Dr. Mac booms as she crosses the railroad tracks carrying a big first aid box and an empty cage.

"Over here!" Maggie calls.

"Dr. Mac, we can't find Socrates. And there's a huge colony of strays living here," I say as she walks over to us. "Some of the neighborhood kids have been feeding them and the parents are upset and think the cats are bad and Animal Control is going to take them away and—"

"One thing at a time, Sunita," Dr. Mac says patiently. "Why don't we take care of this guy first, and you can tell me the rest back at the clinic."

I nod. She's right.

I'm not sure how old Dr. Mac is. Fifty-five, or maybe sixty. It wouldn't be polite to ask. Except for her white hair, it's hard to believe she's a grandmother. She runs marathons and wears blue jeans and T-shirts from the Gap. Along with running the clinic, she writes a newspaper column about pets and travels all over the world giving lectures. But what really matters, I guess, is that she has lots of energy, she's smart, and she's great with animals and kids. And she's the best person to have around in an emergency.

Dr. Mac kneels in the dirt about a foot away from the injured cat. "Do you know how this happened?" she asks.

We crouch down next to her. "He was hit by a car yesterday," I explain. "A boy saw it happen. He said the cat won't eat or drink anything."

"That's not good," Dr. Mac says as she looks the cat over from head to paws. Why isn't she touching him? I've never seen her examine any animal without at least checking its pulse.

"Do you want me to hold him?" I ask. That's one of my favorite jobs at the clinic, holding cats during examinations.

"Sorry, Sunita," Dr. Mac replies. "You can't help with this one. Matter of fact, I want both of you to back up a little, well out of the reach of this critter."

"Why?" Maggie asks. "It's just a stray cat."

Dr. Mac shakes her head. "This isn't an ordinary

stray. This looks like a feral cat. Strays are cats that have been raised around humans, so they're used to being touched. Feral cats are born and raised in the wild. Some people call them wild cats, though they are obviously different from true wildcats like cougars or panthers. The proper word for them is *feral*. They hate being touched by people. They think of us as predators, something that will hurt them."

Maggie and I exchange surprised looks. Can this be true? I know that some cats have to live outside, but I can't imagine a cat that wouldn't like Dr. Mac. Or me.

Dr. Mac opens the equipment box and takes out what looks like a giant pair of oven mitts. "This guy could be infected with any number of diseases. I guarantee he'll try to scratch or bite me," she says, putting on the mitts. "I'm going to need these just to get him in the cage."

As she picks up the blanket the cat is lying on, he jerks his neck and sinks his teeth into the nearest mitt.

"See?" she says. "The best thing to do is to get him into the clinic as soon as possible. Once we're there, I'll give him a sedative to calm him down. Then I'll be able to examine him. Safely." She puts the feral cat in the cage, closes the door, then quickly drapes a big towel over the cage.

"Why did you cover it?" I ask.

"So he'll feel more secure," Dr. Mac says, taking off the protective mitts. "You didn't find Socrates?"

"No," I say sadly. "And he's hurt, Dr. Mac. You should have seen the cut on his leg."

"Zoe told me what happened." She sighs heavily. "I've seen him chase cats out of the yard before, but he always comes right back."

She looks like she's about to say more, but she stops herself. She's probably thinking about all the dangerous things a cat can run into: cars, dogs, poisonous plants. No—I can't let myself think about it. We'll find him. We have to.

"David and Brenna are asking around to see if anyone has seen him. We know he came this way," Maggie explains.

Dr. Mac looks around, then checks her watch. "If he doesn't show up by tomorrow, you kids can make up some flyers with his picture and hand them out. We have to get back to the clinic now. Go find Brenna and David, and meet me at the van."

She picks up the cage, and the cat inside it meows.

"We're leaving? What about the other cats

around here?" I ask. "Mrs. Frazier said the Animal Control people were going to round them up tomorrow. She made it sound like they were all going to be put to sleep! What if they capture Socrates, too?"

"We'll talk about it at the clinic, Sunita," Dr. Mac says. "I promise."

When we get to the clinic, the other kids head to the kitchen for a snack. I follow Dr. Mac into the exam room.

Dr. Mac sets the cage with the feral cat in it on the metal exam table, then she prepares a sedative. She takes a small glass vial out of the refrigerator and sets it on the counter. Next, she takes a syringe out of a drawer. She sticks the needle of the syringe through the rubber cap of the vial and draws out a little of the liquid sedative.

"This will relax him and take the edge off the pain he's suffering. Then we'll be able to see what's going on."

"Aren't you going to take him out of the cage first?" I ask.

Dr. Mac shakes her head. "Not until he's medicated. I can't examine him wearing those protective mitts, and I don't like being bitten."

She walks around the table until she's standing behind the caged cat.

"I want you to stand where he can see you, but stay far away. I don't want him to stick his paw out between the bars and scratch you. Call to him. Distract him so I can get this done."

The cat's ears are flicking forward and backward as he tries to hear what is going on around him and keep track of where we both are.

"Here, kitty, kitty, kitty," I call, making a squeaking noise. "Over here, sweetie. Look at me."

Out of the corner of my eye, I can see Dr. Mac ready to stick the needle through the bars of the cat carrier. The cat turns his head and looks at Dr. Mac. He struggles to his feet.

"No, no, over here," I say in a high-pitched voice. "Kitty, stay still."

Dr. Mac raises the needle.

"Kitty, kitty!"

His eyes are on me. Dr. Mac sticks the needle in the cat's rump.

"Fssst!" The cat turns, and fast as lightning shoots a paw through the bars.

"Ouch!" cries Dr. Mac. "He got me!" She drops the syringe on the floor and holds her hand. Already a thick line of blood is oozing from the long scratch.

"Oh, no! Are you OK?" I ask.

Dr. Mac takes a deep breath and walks over to the sink. She turns on the hot water and squeezes soap on the cut.

"He got me good," she says as she scrubs the wound. "This scratch is pretty deep. That's why I get my shots every other year. Even if he's carrying a disease like rabies, my vaccinations will keep me safe."

"Are you going to need antibiotics, too?" I ask.

"Spoken like a true doctor's daughter," Dr. Mac answers. "If this were a bite, I would. But I'll put some antibiotic cream on it and it should be fine."

"I can't believe how fast he moved," I say.

She turns off the water. "That's how cats are. A dog will usually give you a sign that he's irritated and might bite. But a cat can turn and attack before you know what's happening." She dries the scratch with a paper towel, spreads the germ-killing cream on the scratch, then covers it with a small bandage.

She looks at our patient, then at her hand. "I think we should call this one Tiger. He's definitely feral, a wild one." She looks me in the eye. "Be careful, Sunita. Feral cats are unpredictable. You always have to be on your guard around them."

"You sound just like Mrs. Frazier. He just needs

some love," I say. "Once he's feeling better, he'll calm down. Then we'll find him a good home."

Dr. Mac shakes her head. "He might look like a house cat to you, but he's not. He was born in the wild, probably to an abandoned or runaway pet. He's been raised wild and doesn't have any interest in being a pet. Now, I could use some gauze and disinfectant here."

I get the supplies she needs from the cupboard. I know I can't say this, but I think she's wrong. Tiger has had a hard life so far, and he just needs some tender, loving care. I could teach him, show him that humans aren't bad. I'm the only person Socrates is willing to cuddle with, and I can calm down our crankiest cat client.

That's what I'll do. I'll take care of Tiger while he's recuperating, help him get used to people. I'll tame him. That will change Dr. Mac's mind and Mrs. Frazier's, maybe even my mother's.

But that won't happen overnight. Animal Control is coming to get the cats in Cat Land tomorrow. We have to find a way to stop them—fast.

"Sunita?" Dr. Mac says to get my attention. "You look like you're a million miles away. We can start the exam now."

The sedative has relaxed the cat so much that Dr. Mac can take him out of the cage and lay him on the table. He doesn't even flick his tail when she starts the exam.

First, she listens to his heart and lungs with a stethoscope. "His heartbeat is strong—a little fast, but that's understandable, given all the stress. Respiratory rate is fast, but I don't hear any wheezing or whistling."

She moves her hands slowly over the cat's legs, back, and stomach.

"No broken ribs—that's good. That leg might be fractured, so we'll X-ray. Hopefully, it's just swollen from the trauma of the accident. If so, he'll just need to stay confined for a while so it can heal. While he's recovering, we'll give him all his shots, and we'll neuter him so he can't go out and make any kittens. There are already too many feral cats out there."

Dr. Mac takes a bag of clear intravenous fluid— an I.V.—from the cupboard, hangs it on a metal stand, and connects some long plastic tubing to it. An I.V. is a mixture of sterile water with important nutrients that injured animals need.

"I'll start the I.V.," she says, inserting a thin plastic needle into a vein in Tiger's foreleg. Then she connects the end of the I.V. tube to the needle, allowing the fluid to flow from the bag into Tiger's vein. "That will rehydrate him and make him feel better," she says as she adjusts the flow of fluid into the tube.

While she's cleaning out the scrapes on Tiger's hip, I tell her about the conversation with Mrs. Frazier.

"She can't get the county to put those cats to sleep, can she?" I ask. "And what about Socrates? He could get captured too."

"Yes, she can," Dr. Mac answers. "The law in every state allows officials to remove animals that pose a danger to the health of people. Mrs. Frazier is probably most concerned about rabies. It is usually seen in foxes, raccoons, skunks, and bats, but domestic animals can get it too. With rabies, you can't be too careful."

"What is rabies, exactly?" I ask.

Dr. Mac tosses a dirty piece of gauze in the trash and takes a clean one. "Rabies is a disease that is passed in saliva, when an infected animal bites another animal or a person. It attacks the nervous system and the brain. When an animal is infected, it becomes very aggressive. It drools and attacks anything that comes close. Rabies can be prevented if a bite victim receives treatment quickly. Without treatment, the victim will die. That's why Mrs. Frazier and her neighbors are so scared."

"But you said you got shots," I say.

She moves on to another raw spot on Tiger's leg that looks really infected. "Animal-care workers get vaccinated because we're around animals all day, every day. It doesn't make any sense for the average person to do that. Instead, the law requires all pets like dogs, cats, and ferrets to be vaccinated. That keeps the animals safe, and their owners, too."

She peels off the latex gloves. "Done. Let's get him into a nice cozy cage in the recovery room before this stuff wears off."

FIVE

The recovery room is where a couple of different things happen. It's where we take animals who have just had surgery, so we can keep an eye on them. It also has our hospital "beds." There are rows of cages built into the far wall, where patients who are still too sick to go home can stay.

Dr. Mac walks over to the cupboard on the far wall and rummages through the top shelf.

"What are you looking for?" I ask.

"This," she answers, holding up a sign that says DANGEROUS ANIMAL. STAY AWAY! She hangs the sign on Tiger's cage.

"That ought to do it," she says.

Tiger blinks his green eyes at me and meows softly.

"He looks so sad," I say.

"He'll be fine," she assures me. "He's in for a

couple of days of rest and recovery. Now, I have a few chores for you and the others to do before you go to the Lakes' house for dinner."

"Dr. Mac, wait," I say as she steps to the door. "I have to ask you something."

She turns. "What, Sunita?"

How do I say this? "It's…Socrates and the other cats. I'm worried about them. Mrs. Frazier says they'll all be taken away, and—you know what that means."

She nods once. Dr. Mac hates it when animals are put to sleep for no good reason.

"Couldn't you talk to her?" I ask. "Convince her to leave the cats alone? We could set up an adoption program like we did for the puppies."

Last month, Maggie tracked down a puppy mill and we rescued all the dogs who were being abused there. Dr. Mac worked with some other vets and the local animal shelter to find homes for all the dogs. I bet we could do the same thing for the cats in Cat Land.

Dr. Mac pulls up a stool and sits down. She taps her finger on the counter for a minute. Finally, she speaks.

"Mrs. Frazier has a very good point, Sunita. The size of that colony will just grow and grow unless something is done. A pair of breeding cats can have a litter of five or six kittens three times a year. And by the time those kittens are six to seven months old, they can have kittens of their own."

I do the math. "Dr. Mac, that means one pair of cats could wind up with eighty kittens in a single year!"

"That explains why Mrs. Frazier is upset, doesn't it? Imagine all those cats living behind your house," she says.

"I'd rather have them living in my house."

Dr. Mac chuckles. "I'm sure you would. But it's not that simple. The life of a stray or feral cat is short and harsh. And it's a huge problem. I just read an article that estimated there are sixty million feral cats in the U.S., as many as there are pet cats. And the number grows every day."

I look past the DANGER sign to Tiger, who has drifted off to sleep. "We can't let Animal Control round them up. We have to find homes for them," I say stubbornly. "We can't leave them out there."

"Your intentions are great, Sunita, but you aren't looking at the facts. There may be a few strays in that group who are used to being around people, but most of them are feral—born wild and will stay wild. You can't turn a feral cat into a house cat."

"None of them will have a chance to be any kind of cat if we don't do something by tomorrow morning," I plead. My heart starts to race. Socrates! What if Animal Control gets him? He could be put to sleep with the other cats. I turn around to face Dr. Mac.

"You're always telling us to make a positive difference. Can't we do it here? Can't we do something to save these cats?"

Dr. Mac taps her finger on the counter again.

"There might be another option," she says slowly.

"What?"

"I've read about a few communities that have been trying TVSR programs."

"What's that? It sounds like a cable TV station."

Dr. Mac smiles. "No, not quite. TVSR stands for Treat, Vaccinate, Spay, and Release. They trap the cats in a colony, like Cat Land, then bring them back to the veterinary clinic. There they sedate them, like we did with our friend Tiger, and give them a complete checkup, treating any infections or injuries they may have. Then they vaccinate the cats against rabies and other diseases. They spay the female cats and neuter the males to keep the population from growing.

"Once they recover from the surgery, the animals

are released. They put a small notch in the cats' ears so people will know they've been treated. They won't reproduce, they won't spread disease, and they get to live out their short lives in peace. As far as I know, we've never tried anything like that around here. Might be worth giving it a shot."

She stands up and slaps her hands on her jeans. "Here's what I'll do. I'll go down to Cat Land in the morning to talk to the Animal Control officers. I know most of them. I'll see if they'll let me try a TVSR program."

"Can we come with you?"

"Don't know why not. It's a Saturday. We could take another look around for Socrates if he hasn't come home by then. But now, there's work to do before you all go to Brenna's. Let's get cracking."

SIX

Ta-da!" Brenna shouts as Mrs. Lake turns the car onto the gravel road that leads to her house.

We drive up to a roomy log cabin. It looks almost magical, with flowers of every size and color blooming, bird feeders hanging from branches, and the smell of pine in the air. The Lakes' property is surrounded on three sides by a nature preserve. It's hard to believe we're in the middle of the suburbs.

"The Lake family estate!" Brenna says with a grin.

"You're so lucky to have a place in the woods," Zoe says.

"It reminds me of Laura Ingalls Wilder's Little House in the Big Woods," I add.

"Or the 'Angry Beavers'!" shouts David, naming one of his favorite cartoons. "They live in the forest, too."

"My mom calls it 'The Hundred-Acre Wood,'" Brenna says. "I think she does that just to embarrass me."

Mrs. Lake looks at us in the rearview mirror of the station wagon. "You used to think that Pooh Bear and Tigger lived next door," she reminds Brenna.

"No, I didn't," Brenna protests.

I believe her mother. Brenna's face is turning deep red.

I like Mrs. Lake. Her chestnut brown hair has silver strands in it that match her silver earrings and bracelets. She works part-time at Golden Age, the retirement community where my grandfather lives.

"I can remember..." Mrs. Lake starts.

"That's enough, Mom," Brenna says quickly. As the car stops in front of the house, she opens her door. "Come on, let me show you around!"

"Don't be long," Mrs. Lake says. "Your dad said he would have dinner ready."

We follow Brenna around back. There are two other small cabins set a short distance behind her house.

"That one is Dad's workshop," Brenna says. "He's a carpenter. He makes furniture."

The double doors of the workshop are open

wide. The walls are lined with tools all neatly hung and organized by size. There are a couple of wood-working machines in the middle of the floor and some beautiful chairs under the window, waiting for customers.

"Don't you love that smell?" Zoe says. The air smells like sawdust.

"You're only saying that because we don't have any skunks right now," Brenna laughs. "Want to see the critter barn?"

The "barn" is where the Lakes keep injured wild animals and nurse them back to health. The Lakes are licensed wildlife rehabilitators. Sick or hurt animals are brought to them, and they nurse the animals back to health. Once the animals have recovered, they are set free. Brenna is really proud that her family does this.

She holds up her hand to stop us before we go in.

"We can't stay in there long. Mom and Dad don't want the animals to get too used to people. And we have to be quiet. If we talk loudly or goof around, that can scare them."

"What do you have in there?" David asks, trying to see through the window over Brenna's shoulder.

"Only a woodchuck and a baby fox right now. The fox arrived yesterday. He hasn't settled in yet.

He got hit by a cart on a golf course. Can you imagine that? Let's go."

We file into the barn silently, pass a few empty pens, and walk to the center of the building. Brenna holds her finger to her lips, then points to a hollow log in one pen.

"Woodchuck," she whispers.

You could have fooled me. The woodchuck must be hiding inside the log. Since there isn't much to look at, we move on.

The baby fox is in the next pen. When he sees us, he skitters into the corner and hides his head, his body shaking. His left back leg is bandaged.

He lifts his head a little to peek at me over his bushy tail, his eyes wide with fright. I wish I could pick him up, stroke his beautiful red fur, and tell him not to worry, everything will be all right.

"We better leave," Brenna whispers.

The Lakes' kitchen table is small, but they've set up a card table at the end of it so we can all sit together. As we take our seats, Brenna introduces us to her father, who has a cheerful bushy beard and one pierced ear. Her older brother Sage and younger brother Jayvee look just like their dad, minus the beard of course.

"Hey, Poe!" Brenna calls. She whistles once and a large black crow hops into the kitchen. He looks at us and tilts his head.

"Everybody, this is Edgar Allan Poe Crow," Brenna says. "He's my buddy." She tosses him the corner of a hamburger roll. Poe snaps it up in his beak and gulps it down.

"Caw!" he cries.

Poe's wing was so badly damaged by gunshot last year that he can't fly any kind of distance. He's the only "critter" that the Lakes have let stay with them permanently.

"Sit down, everybody," Mr. Lake says as he carries the food to the table. "Let's eat."

While we feast on hamburgers and the best homemade potato salad I have ever eaten, Brenna tells her parents about Socrates' disappearance and what we found in Cat Land.

"I'm sure Dr. MacKenzie's cat will come home in a day or two," Mrs. Lake reassures us. "From what Brenna has told us, he sounds like an independent, smart animal."

"Yes, but he was hurt in that fight," Maggie points out. "If his wounds get infected, he won't have the energy to come home."

"He's only been gone a few hours," Mr. Lake says. "I wouldn't be too worried yet."

"I hope you're right," I say. "That's pretty much what Dr. Mac said. Seeing the strays really scared me, though. What if we never find Socrates and he ends up living outside? What will he do when it snows?"

"Well, the size of that colony of strays should prove it's a good place to live," Mrs. Lake says as she passes the potato salad down to David. "I had no idea it was so large. I had heard that there were only a few cats there."

"I wish we could rescue all of them," I say. "I'd love to take one home."

"I don't think they need rescuing," says Sage. "Those strays have survived without much help."

"But they shouldn't have to," I say hotly. "It's not fair for them to have to live like that."

"Maybe, maybe not," says Mr. Lake. "It can be hard to tell when it's right for people to interfere in the life of a wild animal."

"Assuming these cats are all feral," Mrs. Lake adds.

"You say they are being fed by that boy and his sister. To me that means they aren't really wild, they're dependent on humans for food," Mr. Lake says.

"Yeah, but what about the bears in Yellowstone National Park?" Sage says. He leans on the table. "They used to eat the garbage left behind by tourists. When the park made sure people cleaned up after themselves, the bears went back to their normal eating habits. They weren't depending on the humans. They were just taking the easiest meal they could find. The cats are doing the same thing."

"But cats are not bears," Zoe says. "Cats are pets. I think Sunita is right. It's not fair that they have to live like that. They all deserve something better."

Brenna's father pulls at his beard. "Now I'll disagree with what Dr. Mac said on one point. There are some people who have brought feral cats into their homes and more or less domesticated them— made them into pets."

"So I'm right," I say.

Mr. Lake shakes his head slowly. "Not exactly. Even those 'domesticated' ferals are nervous around people. I know a woman who has done this a few times. She said it took her cat more than a year to get used to being in the same room as her. And it still won't sit in her lap or let her pet it."

"That sounds like Socrates," Zoe says. "Maybe he's really feral. The only people he lets near him are Sunita and Gran."

Maggie points toward her cousin. "Wait a minute—that black cat, the one that fought with Socrates. She's pregnant," she explains to Brenna's family. "What about her kittens? Will they be feral or tame?"

Brenna's mother shrugs. "If they are raised outside, without people, they'll be feral. That's why feral cat colonies are such a problem. First you have cats that quickly reproduce, and second, they aren't socialized as pets. There's not much that can be done about them."

"Except to round them up and kill them," Brenna says bitterly.

"I know that sounds harsh, Brenna," her father says gently. "But you've seen the results of overpopulation. When you have too many of one species in one place, nature takes care of it. They run out of food, the weak die. Putting them to sleep is much more humane."

The table goes silent as everyone thinks about that.

"Actually, there is something that we can do for the cats," I say. They all look at me. "Dr. Mac told me about it this afternoon. It's called a TVSR program."

By the time I finish explaining how the program works, we've cleared away the dishes and started on dessert.

"Dr. Mac promised she would talk to the Animal Control people tomorrow. That's when they're supposed to round up the cats."

"I've never heard of TVSR, but it makes sense," Mrs. Lake says. "And the animals are released back where they were found?"

"That's what bothers me," I say. "I hate the idea of forcing them to live on their own again. I want to find people to adopt them after they've been treated."

Sage takes another brownie from the platter. "Wouldn't work. You heard Dad. A wild animal is a wild animal."

"What about Poe?" Brenna challenges him.

The two of them argue about whether Poe is wild or tame, but I'm not really listening. I'm still back on what Mr. Lake said about his friend who tamed a feral cat.

I'll start with Tiger tomorrow. It's just a matter of being patient, and I can be patient. Cats that were raised in the wild need extra love and understanding. Maybe Socrates was a feral kitten. Dr. Mac told me she found him wandering around the

yard when he was tiny. I was able to win his heart.
I can do the same thing with Tiger and the others—
I'm sure of it.

SEVEN

I'm a little late getting to the clinic. On Saturdays, I have an early ballet lesson, and today it ran long.

Walking up the sidewalk to the front door of the clinic, I feel as if something's wrong. What is it? I changed out of my ballet clothes. Mother knows where I am. The clinic looks normal, even though there aren't many clients' cars parked in the driveway. What's missing?

Socrates.

This is where he usually greets me. A lump grows in my throat, and I try to swallow it. Dr. Mac and Mrs. Lake both said he'd be home soon, but he's not. If Maggie and Zoe have those flyers ready, we can spread them all over the neighborhood today. We'll find him. We have to find him.

As I walk in, the others are clustered around the

reception counter. Dr. Mac is trying to listen to the person on the other end of the telephone.

"Yes," she says into the phone loudly. "Yes, we are missing a cat."

Maggie jumps up and down. "Someone found Socrates!"

"Shh!" her grandmother says. "You live near the Fraziers?"

It has to be him!

"When can we pick him up?" Maggie asks.

"Is he OK?" I ask.

"Wait a minute," Dr. Mac says. "What does the cat look like?" she asks the person on the other end of the line.

We wait. Dr. Mac nods once, twice.

"Are you sure?"

She's not smiling anymore.

"Well, thank you for checking. I'm afraid it's not ours. Good-bye." She hangs up the phone and turns to us. My heart sinks.

"The cat she found is orange, but it's small, about seven or eight pounds. It has white ears, and it's a female. Sorry, it's not Socrates."

"Guess it's a good thing we made these flyers after all," Maggie says glumly. She waves a stack of neon yellow paper. Printed on the front is MISSING

CAT and a picture of Socrates sitting on Dr. Mac's desk.

"We'll find him, don't worry," Dr. Mac says. "Let's get in the van."

✚

It's a quick drive to Dorset Street, the closest road to Cat Land. Dr. Mac tries to fill the silence in her car by telling us about the Animal Control officer we'll be meeting.

"There he is," she mutters, as she parks along the street. A tall, slim man wearing a dark green shirt and matching pants is leaning over some papers on the hood of a red pickup truck with ANIMAL CONTROL painted on the door.

"Dr. MacKenzie," he says as Dr. Mac walks over to shake his hand. The five of us trail behind her. "What are you doing here?" he asks.

"Good morning, Gary," she says. "You've never met my granddaughters, have you? This is Maggie and this is Zoe, and behind them are some of my clinic volunteers—Sunita, Brenna, and David. Everyone, this is Gary Snyder."

He looks puzzled at the sudden appearance of a veterinarian and five sixth-graders. We all say polite hellos.

Dr. Mac sticks her hands in the pockets of her blue jeans. "I must have left fifty messages on your answering machine late yesterday, Gary."

"Sorry about that, Doc," the Animal Control officer answers. "We were out on a bat call. A woman found a whole bunch of bats in her attic, and we had to get them out." He shudders. "I don't like bats. They give me the creeps."

"Yech," Zoe says with disgust.

"Bats are useful. They eat mosquitoes," Brenna points out.

"I'll just use bug spray, thanks," Zoe says.

"It took a while, but we got them all out," Gary continues. "I didn't get a chance to check my messages. Sorry if you were trying to get me. What brings you out this way?" he asks Dr. Mac. "A house call?"

"Hardly," Dr. Mac answers. "I think we're here for the same reason." She nods toward the railroad tracks and the clearing beyond. "Those cats."

Gary frowns slightly. "Those are feral cats, Dr. MacKenzie. The neighbors here are in an uproar. I've got to take them out."

"And do what with them?" Brenna asks hotly.

"I'll take care of this, Brenna," Dr. Mac says.

As she explains the TVSR program to Gary, I

keep my fingers crossed behind my back. I hope he agrees to it. Dr. Mac told me in the van that if he says no, there is nothing more she can do. As an Animal Control officer, it's his job to make decisions about the safety of people and animals.

Dr. Mac finishes her explanation. Gary glances up the street. No kids are outside playing yet.

"And who's paying for all this?" he asks. "The cost of the vaccines, surgery, and medicine is going to add up quickly. You know there's no extra money in my budget."

Dr. Mac looks over at us. I cross my toes inside my sneakers.

"I won't charge the county," she says. "I'll do it for free and consider it a contribution to the community."

Gary rubs the back of his neck. "And they won't be able to spread anything?"

"That's right," Dr. Mac says.

We all nod, five heads bobbing up and down in perfect rhythm.

Dr. Mac walks to the van and brings back a thick binder, which she hands to Gary.

"I put together some information for you. I figured you would want to read up on it yourself. These studies say that in areas where TVSR is being used, the cat population has decreased slowly and steadily. Some towns have reduced their feral cat population by half after running TVSR programs for a few years."

"And you want me to release the cats back here?" Gary says. He doesn't look convinced. "The neighborhood association will have my head."

"If the colony is removed, other feral cats will take it over and the neighbors will be at risk for disease again. TVSR works better. The statistics are very convincing. But you'll have to do some educating. Have a meeting with the residents. I'd be happy to speak to them if you want."

Gary flips through the pages in the notebook with a frown. I'm squeezing my crossed fingers and toes so hard they are getting numb.

"Please," I say. "Please let us try this. These cats need our help. We could save their lives. Please."

I swallow hard. I'm not used to speaking out like that, especially in front of Animal Control officers.

Gary takes a deep breath. "Well, I've always hated putting these guys to sleep. It's not their fault." He glances at the Fraziers' house. "I'll do it. We'll try the program this one time, to see if it works. And I'll set up a meeting to explain it to the neighbors. But if this doesn't work, we'll have to do it the other way. I won't have a choice."

"Thank you very much!" I say with a big grin.

"Thanks," Dr. Mac says. "It will be good to work together."

He places the binder on the front seat of his truck. "So we need to round up a bunch of them for you to take back, huh? Want to use my traps?"

"Traps?" I say. "We're going to trap them? That sounds horrible. Won't that hurt them?"

Gary laughs. "It's not that kind of trap," he says, reaching for something in the back of the pickup. "This is a humane trap. Let me show you how it works."

The trap looks like a big cat carrier, but its sides can slide back and forth to hold the caged animal still, squeezing it gently when the vet is trying to give a shot.

"We usually have to give wild animals a sedative before we treat them," Gary explains. "You would not believe the fuss they can put up."

I'd put up a big fuss too if someone trapped me in a metal box, but I don't say that. Once we get these cats taken care of, maybe I'll design a better trap. That would be a great project for the school science fair.

Dr. Mac lifts her bandaged hand. "Wish I'd had

one of those yesterday," she says.

"We'll make sure no one gets hurt," Gary promises. "How many do you want to trap today?"

"I can handle about six at a time at the clinic," Dr. Mac replies. "I brought some nice, smelly tuna to stick inside the traps."

"That will bring them running," he says. "I'll start setting these up."

Dr. Mac turns to us. "I don't think this will take too long. Why don't you start passing out flyers?"

"Sounds like a plan. C'mon, guys," Maggie says.

"Is it OK if I stay to watch?" I ask Dr. Mac. "I might see Socrates."

"All right, Sunita," Dr. Mac says as she takes one of the traps out of Gary's pickup. "You'll be our observer. But you are here to watch, not to touch. Got it?"

"Yes, ma'am," I say.

We cross over the railroad tracks to Cat Land. It's deserted, but I can feel the eyes watching us from the tall grass.

A curtain moves in the Fraziers' window, but I can't see who is watching us. I wish I could go in and explain to Jamie what we're doing, but his mom might not understand. I hope his mom goes to Gary's meeting.

"Sunita, why don't you sit over there?" Dr. Mac says as Gary sets up the traps. She points to some broken slabs of concrete piled at the edge of the clearing.

Gary nods to Dr. Mac. The traps are all set. The two of them walk to the opposite side of the clearing and crouch down out of sight. I sit as still as a mouse.

It takes a few minutes, but the cats appear, slinking out of the weeds and slithering out of the boxcar, their noses twitching in the air, trying to trace that tantalizing tuna smell. We saw a lot of these cats yesterday—the gray with the broken tail, the black-and-white young cats. But no Socrates. They circle the traps warily. I bet they suspect something is wrong. Will they go inside the funny-looking things for a treat?

Something brushes by my hand. A fly. I flick my hand to make it go away. It lands again, tickles my hand. I look down.

Oh, my gosh. There she is, sitting right next to me—Mittens, the soon-to-be mom cat that fought with Socrates! I glance around quickly, but there's no sign of our feisty orange clinic cat. I just know he followed her here after their fight. Maybe he'll come out, too, if he smells that tuna.

Mittens tilts her black head back and looks me in the eye. I bet I know what she's thinking—*Where have you been? I've been waiting.*

I squint. Hidden under the fur on her neck is a black flea collar. Wait—that means Mittens isn't a feral cat after all. She was abandoned! She used to have people who loved her, and now she's all alone. She's not wild, she's domesticated—a house cat who wants to live inside and sleep on bedspreads. She's safe.

I know Dr. Mac told me not to touch any of these cats, but I can't help myself. Mittens is probably used to people. Will she let me touch her? She won't scratch me, I just know it. I reach my fingers out slowly.

Mittens bumps her head against my hand.

She likes me!

I scratch between her ears and she starts to purr. She rubs the edge of her mouth against my knuckles. This is great! I wish I could pick her up.

Bang!

A trap in the clearing swings shut, locking a cat inside. *Bang! Bang! Bang!* Three more traps close.

Mittens looks around, not sure what to do. The

trapped cats howl in outrage, and Mittens runs off before I can stop her, disappearing into that green tangle of bushes and weeds. I'll never find her in there.

EIGHT

Back at the clinic, Dr. Mac warns me to stand at the far end of the room before she starts to treat the first cat. I think she's being too careful. The cat is in a cage, after all. But I do what she tells me.

She sedates him, just like she did Tiger, but it is a lot easier to do with the special Animal Control cage. The cat protests with a loud "me-oww!" but quickly relaxes as the medicine takes effect. Dr. Mac relaxes then, too.

"OK, you can come closer if you want," she says. "He's not going anywhere for a while." She opens the trap and lifts out our patient. "On second thought, you may not want to come closer—this cat is crawling with fleas."

Our first TVSR patient is a scrawny, light gray male cat. Dr. Mac quickly checks his heart, lungs, and temperature, and feels his body for bumps or bone problems. She peeks in his mouth.

"Whew! Bad breath. I bet he has an infection in there somewhere. We'll deal with that under anesthetic. Can you get me a tube of antiseptic cream?"

I bring the cream and some gauze, too.

Dr. Mac squeezes the cream onto the gauze pad and gently wipes it on an infected, swollen paw. "That will feel better when you come around," she murmurs.

"Is that all you have to do?" I ask.

"I wish it were, but it's not."

Once the paw is cleaned up, Dr. Mac draws blood for tests and vaccinates the cat for rabies and other cat diseases. She adds a long-acting antibiotic injection to fight off infection. Then she sprays on a flea killer.

"I'll operate on him once he's hydrated," she says. "We'll neuter him so he won't father any kittens. As soon as he's recovered, we'll take him back to where we found him."

"Do you have to?" I ask. "Maybe he'll get used to people if he's around us."

"Believe me, after three days living here, he'll be more than ready to leave."

Dr. Mac wraps the cat in a towel and hands him to me. "Why don't you tuck him in for me? Put him in the row of cages in the corner. I'll go fetch the next feral patient."

After I put the sedated cat in a cage, I peek in on Tiger. He is wide awake today, his ears twitching as he watches me carefully.

Dr. Gabe, the clinic's associate vet, walks in holding an injured parrot. "Don't get too close to that cat," he warns. "Tiger there has quite a reach!"

"He looks a lot better," I say.

"I'll say," Dr. Gabe chuckles.

He opens the door to a birdcage. "Now stay in there and take it easy," he tells the parrot. "You are not a dog. You should not be attacking the mailman."

The parrot steps off his arm and onto the perch.

"What's wrong with him?" I ask.

"He keeps flying into the window in his family's living room whenever the mailman walks up the sidewalk. We thought he might have a broken wing, but the X ray was negative. His folks will be picking him up soon. My prescription is to either move his cage or close the curtains." He pauses. "I was going to tell you something. What was it?"

"Tiger?" I suggest.

He snaps his fingers. "Exactly. You should see the hole he put in my lab coat! That cat has claws of steel and a wicked temper."

I peer in through the metal bars of Tiger's cage. He is sitting with his front paws tucked under him. The I.V. is gone. That means he has enough fluids in his body. He looks a lot better than he did yesterday. Dr. Mac must have bathed and groomed him while he was under the anesthetic for surgery. He almost looks like a different cat. He sure sounds like one—he's purring a happy tune. I can just imagine what he would look like stretched out on my bed.

"All right, I'm outta here," Dr. Gabe says.

"Where are you going?" I ask.

"Out to Lucas Quinn's stables. He has a horse with an injured hoof." He peers into the parrot's cage. "At least he didn't get it trying to scare away the mailman," he tells the bird.

"Br-awk! Fresh boy! Fresh boy!" the parrot squawks as Dr. Gabe heads out the door. When the door closes behind him, Tiger starts to talk to me.

"Mee-row!" he wails.

I know Dr. Mac told us not to touch any of the strays, but I can't help it. Mittens was so friendly to me at Cat Land. I know Tiger will be, too. Now's my chance to get to know him.

I reach out my hand toward the cage a little.

Tiger sniffs the air, then he pulls himself forward until his head is up against the bars. He presses his nose against them so he can smell my fingers. I figure that's a good sign—he wants to be friends.

"Meee-ow!"

What a pitiful sound. He's so lonely!

Part of me knows this is wrong, but I can't help it. Tiger needs some love. Mittens let me pet her— she stayed perfectly calm. Tiger is still recovering from his injury. Even if he wanted to, he couldn't hurt me.

I unhook the latch and open the cage door a tiny bit. Tiger doesn't move. I open it a bit farther and slip my hand inside. He leans forward so I can scratch his head. He's purring louder. I'll just pet him a bit, then close the cage.

"That's a good kitty. I'm not going to hurt you." I move my fingertips down the back of his head. Socrates loves to be scratched like this.

Tiger stops in mid-purr, whips his head around quickly, and locks his teeth on my hand between my thumb and first finger. He bites me hard!

"Ouch!" I shout. "Let go!"

I shake my hand to get him to release it. He pulls back and I slam the door closed and hook the latch.

I'm shaking. I've never been bitten before. The

bite is deep and bloody and really, really hurts! The tears come, I can't stop them. In his cage, Tiger licks his front paw as if nothing has happened.

"Sunita!" Dr. Gabe calls as he runs up the hall. "Are you OK? I thought I heard a shout."

"I'm OK," I say, trying to control my voice and hide my hand.

"What happened? Tell me."

Even if it's going to get me in trouble, I have to show him. I sniff and hold out my hand.

"Oh, no." He grabs some paper towels to clean up the blood. "Tiger?"

"Tiger," I admit. I use my good hand to wipe the tears off my face. My hand is throbbing, and it feels really hot.

He quickly slips on a pair of latex gloves, then washes the wound over the sink.

"We're going to have to call your parents," he says as he pours antiseptic on it. "Sorry if this hurts. We have to kill the germs."

"Oh, no, please don't. I mean, don't call my parents. I'll be fine, really. Just give me a Band-Aid. My mother already hates cats. If she sees this, she'll never let me near one again!"

Dr. Gabe turns off the water and dries my hand.

"You don't understand," he says gravely.

"Animal bites have to be checked out by a doctor. A people doctor. You have to go to the hospital, Sunita. Right now."

NINE

My parents rush through the door of County General Hospital's emergency room. They look around frantically, then spot Dr. Mac and me near the receptionist's desk.

"Oh, Sunita!" Mother runs to me, throws her arms around me for a tight hug, then steps back so she can see me. "Show me."

Daddy hugs me too and kisses my forehead. "Let's see."

I slowly lift my arm to show them my red, swollen hand. Mother gasps.

"It's—it's not that bad," I stammer.

Daddy takes the hand gently in his. "It's deep," he says, frowning.

"It's just a little bite," I say. "Don't get upset."

My parents are usually calm during medical emergencies. Daddy is a cardiologist, a heart doctor, and Mother is an orthopedist. She takes care of broken bones. They're both used to being around injured and sick people.

One time we came across an accident on the highway, and they helped pull two people out of a car, then gave them artificial respiration until the ambulance arrived. That didn't bother them at all. But now they both look pale and very worried. I guess when the injured patient is your own kid, you feel a little different.

"They said a doctor will see her in a minute," Dr. Mac says.

"How did this happen, Dr. MacKenzie?" Mother asks.

"It was all my fault," I interrupt. "Please don't blame Dr. Mac. She warned me to stay away from the wild cats."

"A wildcat caused this?" Mother asks, her voice going up. "A cougar?"

"No," I say. "It was Tiger."

"You were bitten by a tiger?" Mother says loudly. Other people turn to stare at us.

"Not a tiger. Not a cougar. A feral cat," Dr. Mac says quickly. "The same as a domestic house cat, but raised without any human contact so it has reverted to a state of wildness. We've just started a program to vaccinate and spay a colony of feral cats, and we have a few in the clinic. One of them bit Sunita."

"It was completely my fault," I repeat. The last thing I want is for Mother to tell me I can't go to the clinic anymore. "I didn't think it would hurt me. It was purring."

Mother doesn't look like she's listening. I think I can forget about ever getting a cat of my own.

"I'll be happy to talk to the doctor who examines her," Dr. Mac says. "Along with an antibiotic, she should be treated for rabies exposure."

"Rabies?" Mother repeats, eyes wide.

Oh, no.

"Dr. Patel. Dr. Patel?" the receptionist calls from the end of the room. "We can see Sunita now."

"I'll wait for you out here," Dr. Mac says to me. There is no spark in her eyes. I know she feels responsible, even though she's not. "Gary will be here soon. I'll fill him in on what happened."

I'm not sure why he's coming, but I'll have to ask later. Time to see the doctor.

We walk down a long hall to a big room that has lots of curtains separating beds. I've seen emergency rooms on television, but I've never been in one before. It reminds me of the clinic—the lighting is bright and everything is clean. The only thing missing is the sound of barking dogs.

A male nurse with a beard who reminds me of Mr. Lake points us to a curtained area. He talks to my parents about boring hospital things as he takes my blood pressure and temperature. I think he's trying to keep us all calm. After he writes down my vital statistics on a chart, he takes a bottle of special disinfectant soap and a small basin out of a cupboard.

"Let's clean this bite up, shall we?" he says cheerfully.

Dr. Gabe already cleaned the bite, and then Dr. Mac did. This hand has never been so clean.

The nurse gently washes the bite, then he lays a piece of gauze over it. My hand feels hot and itchy.

"Dr. Juarez will be here in just a minute," he says, standing. As he leaves, he pulls the curtain closed to give us some privacy.

Mother strokes my hair. She looks more worried than I've ever seen her. "It's my fault," she says. "I should never have agreed to let you work around animals at the clinic. They're dangerous. This proves it."

"Now, Kamala," Daddy says in a soothing tone of voice. "Let's not get carried away. Things happen to children. They get broken bones and bumps all the time. You'd be out of a job if they didn't!"

Mother has to smile about that. Most of her patients are kids who have fallen off a trampoline or broken an arm while in-line skating.

"You may have a point about bumps and bruises," she says. "But this proves what I've always said about cats: You can't trust them. They are sneaky and dangerous."

I'm not going to get a cat for the next three lifetimes, I just know it.

Dr. Juarez pulls aside the curtain. He's wearing a tie with pictures of Tweety Bird on it. That makes me smile, a little.

"Hello, Kamala, Ravi," he says to my parents.

Good. They all know each other. Maybe having one of their friends treat me will make my parents relax.

He puts on a fresh pair of latex gloves, just like Dr. Mac does before she examines a patient. He sits on a stool and rolls it over to the bed where I'm sitting. He smiles at me warmly.

"I need to take a look at this," he says. "I will try to be gentle, but it may hurt a little. OK?" he asks.

I nod.

He lifts the gauze from the bite and studies the holes made by Tiger's teeth.

"You were truly chomped, my dear," Dr. Juarez says. "Can you move your fingers for me?"

That's not a problem. I open and close my fingers easily.

"Good." Dr. Juarez turns so he can see Mother and Daddy. "I don't see any evidence of damage to nerves or to the bones of her hand," he says. "Sometimes the bite of a dog can break a finger, but that rarely happens with cats. Their jaws aren't strong enough. And puncture wounds don't need stitches."

Mother and Daddy nod.

"I met Dr. MacKenzie outside," Dr. Juarez continues, "and the man from the county animal department—Snyder, Gary Snyder. The cat was vaccinated only yesterday, so we have no way of knowing whether or not it has rabies. We have some decisions to make. I assume she had her last tetanus vaccination when she was six years old? Then she'll need a booster today, as well as an antibiotic."

"Two shots?" I ask.

He pauses to look at me. "You need both. Cat

bites are very deep. I can pretty much guarantee you have some nasty germs in that wound," he explains. "We also have to think about rabies. Dr. MacKenzie says she vaccinated the cat before Sunita got bitten, but the shot may not have had time to take effect. I'll ask her to have the cat tested immediately."

Mother covers her mouth with her hand, like she's holding something in.

"It's OK, Kamala," Dr. Juarez says. "Over seventy percent of rabies cases are transmitted through raccoons and skunks, and another large percentage comes from bats. The chances of this cat having rabies are very, very small."

"And if the animal is negative, she won't need rabies shots?" Daddy asks.

"Wait a minute," I say, remembering something I read once. "How exactly will they test Tiger?"

Dr. Juarez hesitates and looks at the tips of his black shoes. "The only way to test for rabies in a suspected animal is by testing the brain tissue." He lowers his voice. "The only way to do that is to kill the animal. It is done very kindly. He'll get an injection and won't feel a thing."

Hot tears spring to my eyes.

"You can't do that!" I blurt out. "It's not fair. It

was my fault. I should never have opened the cage and tried to pet him." Tears run down my cheeks, and I look at my parents. "I'm sorry."

"You would rather have rabies shots than have this cat—this cat owned by nobody—put to sleep?" Daddy asks.

Dr. Juarez hands me a tissue, and I wipe my tears.

"It doesn't matter who owns him," I say. "I can't let him be killed because I was stupid. Dr. Mac had a giant sign on his cage warning us not to get close, and Dr. Gabe said something too. Can't you see? It's wrong to kill him."

"There is another way to proceed," Dr. Juarez says. "The animal can stay in quarantine, under observation. If it doesn't show any signs of rabies after ten days, then it is not infected. It would not have to be killed."

"Really?" I ask.

"But in the meantime, you would still have to receive two shots tonight, and one more next week. If he's infected, you would need three more after that."

"That's a lot," I say. "Why don't we just wait until the ten days are up? If he has it, then I would start the shots."

"That could be too late for you," Dr. Juarez

explains. "We need to start treatment immediately to be safe."

"If Sunita's infected, will the shots prevent rabies from developing?" Daddy asks.

"Absolutely," Dr. Juarez promises. "Remember— the chance that Sunita is infected is very small, but we're always extremely cautious with rabies. Thousands of people every year get these shots."

Mother looks at Dr. Juarez and then back at me.

"No," I say. "Don't say it."

"Say what?" she asks.

"Don't say that you want Tiger killed," I say. "I'll take the shots."

We go back and forth a few times, my parents trying every way they know to get me to change my mind. But in the end, I win. Tiger will get his chance to live.

Dr. Juarez cleans the skin on my right arm near the shoulder and gives me the first injection.

I take a sharp breath. "Oooo!"

"Are you going to make it?" Daddy asks.

I nod. It doesn't hurt as much as when Tiger bit me.

Dr. Juarez gives me three more shots—one in the right arm, two in the left. I'm feeling a little like a pincushion.

"That's it." Dr. Juarez pulls off the latex gloves

and tosses them in the trash. "All done. You'll need to take antibiotics at home for a week and watch the wound for signs of an infection, but with two docs in the house, that shouldn't be a problem."

"Thank you," I say politely.

"I'll see you," he says to my parents. "Never a dull moment in the E.R."

Dr. Mac and Gary Snyder are waiting for us in the waiting room. We sit down to explain what happened.

"I decided to get the shots," I say. "I didn't want them to kill Tiger."

"She was very firm about this," Daddy says. "Is it true that you will watch him for ten days?"

"Exactly," Gary says. "I'm in the middle of filling out a report on this. We have to follow up on every suspected rabies case. You may get some calls from reporters. Rabies stories are always big news, even if they turn out to be nothing."

"As long as Sunita is safe, that's all that matters," Daddy says, putting his arm around my shoulder and squeezing.

"Ouch!" I squeak. "My shoulder—the shots."

"Sorry, honey." Daddy kisses my forehead.

Dr. Mac looks miserable. "I can't apologize enough, Dr. Patel. I feel responsible for this."

Daddy shakes his head. "Please. Don't give it a moment's thought. Sunita was firm about that as well. She says she ignored your instructions."

Mother presses her lips together tightly. I don't think this is a good time to ask if we can adopt one of the strays. That time may never come. What a horrible day this has turned out to be.

The automatic door at the other end of the room whooshes open, and we all turn to look. An intense-looking woman rushes in carrying a pencil and a slim notebook. She strides over to us.

"We got a call from Animal Control about a rabies victim," she says, glancing first at Gary's green uniform and then at me. "Are you the little girl who was attacked by a vicious wild cat?"

TEN

Vicious wild cat...vicious wild cat... The words of the reporter keep echoing in my head.

I'm trapped in a nightmare of angry cats, six feet tall, with shaggy fur, sharp claws, and pointed teeth. I try to run from them, but no matter where I go, I'm trapped. The cats are coming closer, closer, and closer... I can't get away!

Suddenly, the nightmare shifts.

I'm the cat.

I stretch out my front paws, trying to run faster than I've ever run before. My whiskers bristle in the wind, sensing what is going on around me. Through my paws, I can feel the vibrations of something chasing me. *Hurry!* My tail lashes, and my ears swivel to try and figure out what's so big and loud—what's trying to hurt me. I glance over my shoulder. Giant humans with huge hands swoop in and grope at me, trying to grab me!

There, ahead—a small, dark cave. I'll be safe there. I swerve and put on a burst of speed, running right into the small hole.

Bang! The trapdoor closes.

They got me. I meow as loud as I can, calling for somebody, anybody to come and rescue me. *Let me out!*

The sound of meowing wakes me. I sit straight up in bed. It's me. I'm the one making the noise.

What a weird dream!

I'm not a cat. I'm not being chased by cats. I flop back on my pillows.

"Sunita?" calls Mother, tapping lightly on my door.

"I'm awake."

"Good thing," Mother says as she walks in. "It's nearly lunchtime. Do you want me to bring up some soup? You can stay in bed if you want. How do you feel?"

"Fine, I guess. And I've had enough sleep, thanks." That dream is still very vivid. "I'll come downstairs to eat."

Mother gives me a quick kiss. "I'll get something ready for you."

I have to change out of my pajamas slowly. My

shoulders hurt from the injections, and my hand is killing me. I wish I could get dressed with my eyes closed. There are cats all over my room—on posters, on covers of the books piled on my nightstand, even on the screensaver of my computer. Every time I see one, it reminds me of my dream and the feeling of being locked up. Is that how a wild cat feels when it is trapped and taken away? Is that how Tiger felt? Is that why he bit me?

It gives me the shivers.

My friends from Wild at Heart visit after lunch.

"Cool—you made it into the newspaper!" David shouts as he runs into the family room, where I'm sitting in front of the TV. I mute the ice-skating competition I'm watching.

"I read it," I say. The reporter who was at the hospital yesterday wrote up the story of what happened to me. The headline read "RABIES SCARE." When I saw it at the kitchen table, I didn't feel like eating anything.

The girls walk in, talking to my mother. My five-year-old brother and sister, Harshil and Jasmine, are hiding in the kitchen, watching everything.

"Hi, Sunita," Maggie says.

"She already saw the article," David says to her.

"Sit down, you guys. Has anyone else called about Socrates?" I ask.

"No. We went back to look for him again this morning," Brenna says. "No luck. But he'll turn up," she adds hastily. "He's probably found a nice person who's feeding him caviar or something. I predict two days."

"What does Dr. Mac think?" I ask.

"Gran is worried," Maggie says. "He's never been gone this long. Somebody could have taken him in, I guess. Or he could be sick—he could have been hit by a…"

"Don't say it!" I interrupt. "I agree with Brenna. Socrates is coming back. We have to be positive."

"Tell us about the hospital," Zoe says. "What did they do to you?"

I tell them all about my trip to the emergency room, trying to make it seem like the shots were no big deal.

"It was very serious," Mother says, contradicting me. "We're keeping Sunita home from school for a few days."

This is silly. I don't need to recover from anything, but Mother and Daddy decided this during the car ride home from the hospital.

"When will she be able to come to the clinic?" Maggie asks.

Mother hesitates, not meeting my eyes. "We need to talk about it."

I shake my head slightly, telling my friends to let it go. "How's Tiger and the other cats from Cat Land?"

Maggie grins. "Loud. Gran and Dr. Gabe operated on all of them last night, and by breakfast time they were feeling well enough to howl. And Sherlock Holmes feels like he has to compete. No dumb cat can make more noise than he can!"

I smiled, thinking of Maggie's basset hound surrounded by a roomful of howling cats.

"It gave me a migraine headache," Zoe says solemnly.

"Did not!" her cousin says, pushing her playfully. "Anyway, they go back to Cat Land on Wednesday, and we'll pick up the next batch. I think Gran really likes doing this."

"Some of the cats are strays," I tell my mother. "Abandoned—isn't that awful? We'd really like to find good homes for them."

"How nice," Mother says flatly. Not the response I was hoping for.

"Mommy, Mommy, can we go now?" Jasmine

calls from the kitchen.

Mother glances at her watch. "I promised to take them to the playground," she says. "It's a beautiful day for a walk."

"Can I come with you?" I ask.

"No. You stay right there on the couch and rest," Mother says.

"We should go, too," Brenna says. "We promised Dr. Mac we wouldn't bug you."

"You're not a bother at all," Mother says. "It was very nice of you to come over. I'm glad Sunita has friends like you."

"Thanks. Well, we better go," Maggie says awkwardly.

"Don't let Dr. Mac give my job to anyone else," I say, half-joking, half-serious.

"You know she won't," David says.

My friends file out the door waving and calling good-bye, followed by Mother, Harshil, and Jasmine. I move the living room couch so I can look out the front windows and watch them leave. Maggie and the others walk in the direction of the clinic, while Mother and the twins grow smaller and smaller as they walk toward Main Street.

I lie down on the soft cushions. I'm kind of tired. Maybe I should take a nap. I wish I had Socrates with me now. He'd climb on top of my stomach, circle twice, then plop down, purring loudly. That would make me feel better.

I try to sleep, but I can't. Every time I close my eyes, I remember what it felt like to be trapped— the look in Tiger's eyes, the look in that baby fox's eyes. I hate this feeling.

I was wrong. There is no way I can turn a feral cat into a pet. If a cat has been raised in the wild, then it is a wild animal. We can do our best to make wild cats safe and prevent them from having kittens, but we can't make them into friendly pets.

The worst thing is that my hope of convincing Mother to let me get a cat was totally ruined the second Tiger bit me. I don't know how I'm going to get her to change her mind about cats now.

I wish Dr. Mac had some information I could give Mother. When she gave the TVSR binder to the Animal Control officer, it made a huge difference.

I fluff a pillow, lie down, and sit up suddenly.

That's it! I don't need Dr. Mac to gather the information for me. I'll write the book myself.

ELEVEN

Even though I feel perfectly fine on Monday morning (no more nightmares!), Mother and Daddy still want me to stay home. I spent two hours convincing them to let me keep volunteering at the clinic, so I'm not going to argue about staying home another day. We're all tired of arguing.

After breakfast I go back up to my room and turn on the computer. It is time to do some serious research. I look for articles about why cats make great pets. I also search for feral cats, wild cats, and anything else I can find to help my case. I even find more information about rabies—what the symptoms are, what animals get infected the most, and other useful bits of information that should help.

It takes two days of typing, but by bedtime on Tuesday, it's ready: a thirty-two-page report, complete with a table of contents, bibliography, and cover page with fancy graphics. I call it "Why Cats Are Great."

As I kiss Mother good night, I set the report on the couch next to her.

"What's this?" she asks. "You don't have a report due at school, do you?"

I shake my head. "You could call this extra credit."

She opens it and scans the table of contents. "Sunita, this is not the time to ask for a cat again, not after what you've been through," she warns.

"Just read it. Please," I answer. "Even after being bitten, I want a cat more than anything. I wish I could make you understand how they make me feel. It's like…they understand me. And I understand them." I glance at the bandage on my hand. "Most of the time. Mother, this means a lot to me. Please read what I've written."

Mother sighs. "You never give up, do you? Well, determination is a very good trait. It got me through medical school. OK, I promise I'll read your report. Now get to bed. Tomorrow is a school day."

Thank goodness for that!

I love school. Some people might think that's weird, but I don't care. I love doing science experiments, getting math problems right, learning about history, and checking out big piles of books from the library. Gym isn't my favorite class in the world, but you can't have everything.

Wednesday just flies by. I have to repeat the story of what happened with Tiger about fifty million times to my classmates and teachers. It doesn't help that my parents made me wear the bandage, even though the swelling around the bite has gone down and it looks better.

Before I know it, the last bell of the day rings, and it's time to go to Wild at Heart.

"We're back here," Dr. Mac calls.

"You go see what they're doing, Sunita," Maggie says. "I have to study for a math test."

The others head for the normal after-school chores—cleaning, organizing, and making sure the cupboards are stocked with supplies. I set my backpack behind the receptionist's counter and walk down the hall.

I knock on the door to the recovery room. "Can I come in?"

"All clear," calls Dr. Mac.

As I open the door, both Dr. Mac and Dr. Gabe

are removing the thick mitts they use for handling the feral cats. Six TVSR patients are prowling inside traveling cages lined up on the examination table.

"I'm back," I say.

"Good, we need you," Dr. Mac says warmly. "You are just in time to say good-bye to our first TVSR graduates. Gary Snyder should be here soon to pick them up."

"Didn't know if we would see you again," teases Dr. Gabe. "Not after you've had a taste of stardom. I cut out the newspaper article about you," he says, grinning. "Sheesh—maybe I should let one of these guys take a taste of me. Then I could see my name in print, too."

"No, you don't want that," I say. "Trust me. And I wish they hadn't written that story at all. It made it sound like all the stray cats are really dangerous."

"The reporter had all the facts correct," Dr. Mac points out.

"Yeah, I know," I admit. "But I still didn't like it. Any news on Socrates?"

Dr. Mac shakes her head. "Nothing. It's like he boarded a bus and left town. But we're keeping our hopes up. You should, too."

"I'll try," I say. "What about Tiger? Where is he?"

"We have him in a quarantine cage upstairs in

Dr. Mac's bathroom," Dr. Gabe explains. "She's the only person allowed near him."

"Is he feeling better?" I ask.

"His leg is healing quickly," Dr. Mac says. "No sign of rabies, either. He'll be ready for release as soon as Animal Control lifts the quarantine."

"That's in six more days, right? Next Tuesday?" I ask.

"You got it," Dr. Mac says as she lifts a traveling cage up onto the exam table. The light gray cat inside meows and paces nervously. There's a small notch in his left ear. That will let others know that he's been vaccinated. "How about you—how do you feel?"

"My shoulders are sore from the shots, and my hand still hurts, but it's a lot better than it was."

"I knew a guy who had to get rabies shots once because he was bitten by his own cat," Dr. Gabe says as he hands a file folder to Dr. Mac. "The cat hadn't been vaccinated, and since she was allowed to wander around outside, the doctor said the guy was at risk. You better believe that cat has gotten her shots every year since then."

Dr. Mac looks up from the file. "I'm always surprised at how many people ignore the reminder cards I send out. It's the law, you know—all cats and dogs have to be vaccinated. Maybe that article will inspire a few of them to get on the ball and bring their pets in. Let's hope so."

She pauses to close the file. "I think I'll devote my next newspaper column to it. In the meantime, Sunita, I want you and the other kids to go through the patient files and make a list of who is overdue for their rabies vaccination. It's time for some gentle reminders."

The kitchen is the best part of Dr. Mac's house. It's so big she has a couch in it. There's also a giant fireplace at the far end of the table. I hope she lights a fire in it this winter. That would be really cozy.

It's almost the perfect picture, the five of us working together around Dr. Mac's kitchen table, with Sherlock dozing under the table and Sneakers, Zoe's puppy, trying to wake him up.

Almost perfect. We're missing one very important cat. The room feels cold without Socrates here. I really miss him. Everyone does, even Sherlock. Maggie says he keeps sniffing all over the house, but he can't find the missing cat.

"Dr. Mac said there's no sign of Socrates," I say.

Zoe glances at the others, then shakes her head

sadly. "He's vanished."

"I think someone took him in," Brenna says.

"But he has an identification collar," Zoe argues. "They would have called."

We sit in glum silence staring at the pile of folders. We can't give up yet. When I was doing the research for Mother, I read about cats that traveled across the whole country to go back home. I'm sure Socrates can make it a few blocks.

"We have to be positive," I say. "That's what my dad says when I'm feeling sad."

"That's very perky of you," Brenna says.

"Hey, where did his bowl go?" I point to the corner where Socrates usually eats from his special "Fat Cat" bowl.

"Gran put it away," Zoe explains. "We were keeping it full of food for Socrates, but the dogs kept eating it. It's in the cupboard."

That makes it seem like he's never coming back. I can feel the lump growing in my throat. *Don't cry, don't pout—do something. Be positive.*

"Let's put the bowl back where it belongs," I say. "We don't have to put any food in it, just leave it in the corner. It will make us feel better."

Maggie smiles at me. "You got it." She jumps up from the table to get Socrates' bowl.

"Are you sure Dr. Mac said we have to check *all* of these files?" David groans as he pulls another from the pile. "This is going to take forever."

"It's not that hard," I say. "We just have to stay organized. Don't mix up the piles of what's been checked and not checked. I bet we can get through the Cs by the time we have to go home."

"No way," Brenna says. "Not if we go with Dr. Mac and Gary to release the cats."

"Are we allowed?" I ask.

"Well, we all got a huge 'You must follow directions or you'll get hurt' lecture from Gran when she got back from taking you to the hospital," Zoe says. "But they said we can watch if we want."

"Sorry about that, guys," I apologize.

"Don't worry about it," Zoe says. "But what about your parents? Your mom seemed a little nervous when we saw you on Sunday. I didn't know if she would let you come back to the clinic."

I nod. "It took some convincing. I've got her reading all this stuff about cats to prove they aren't the horrible beasts she imagines. Believe it or not, I'm still trying for a cat of my own. She said she liked my determination. Anyway, I really want to see the release. I bet the feral cats will be really happy to be outside again," I say. "They've been cooped up here for a long time."

"Wait a minute," Brenna says, laying down her pencil. "I thought you were the one who said all cats need a home."

A blush creeps up my neck. "I wasn't thinking about what the cats felt like when I said that. Dr. Mac was right. The ferals belong outside, where they're used to living."

"Wow," Brenna says. "I never thought I'd hear you say that."

"I hope we can capture Mittens this time," Maggie says. "It would be great if we could find homes for her kittens."

"Too bad Mrs. Frazier was so angry," Zoe says. "Her kids would love a kitten."

"Pigs will fly before that happens," Maggie replies.

We sort through the files in silence, making lists of clients to contact about overdue vaccinations. Suddenly, Sherlock lets out a deep "woof!"

"Someone's here," Maggie says without looking up from her pile.

David peeks through the blinds. "It's Gary. Time to release the cats."

TWELVE

Cat Land is quiet and peaceful when we arrive. We follow Gary and Dr. Mac to the clearing. When Gary opens the doors of the first two cages, the cats race out and disappear into the weeds.

"Later, dudes," David calls to the cats.

"They sure look like happy campers, don't they?" Gary says.

Dr. Mac grins. "You look pretty pleased yourself."

Gary crosses his arms over his chest and studies the spot where the cats hurried into the underbrush. "Yep. I became an animal control officer because I wanted to help animals. I really like the way this is working out."

I think we should be videotaping this. Lots of people think animal control officers are the bad guys, like the old-fashioned dogcatchers in cartoons. But Gary obviously cares about animals.

"Uh-oh," Maggie says. "Here comes trouble."

Mrs. Frazier is headed toward us, punching numbers on a cell phone. She looks even angrier than she did the first time I met her.

"What do you think you're doing?" she demands with a red face. "You're supposed to be taking the cats out of here, not bringing more in! Is that why this whole thing is taking so long? You take away a few cats to calm me down, then you sneak more back in? Well, I'm not feeling very calm, Mr. Snyder, not at all!"

"Mrs. Frazier, let me explain," Gary says. "The cats we just released are vaccinated and spayed. They present no danger to you or your family. Mrs. Frazier?"

"Hello? Animal Control?" she says into the cell phone. "Get me the supervisor. We have an emergency."

"Mrs. Frazier, this is not an emergency," Gary tries again. "If you would just listen to me…"

She covers the mouthpiece of the phone with her hand. "No, you listen to me! I will not have my kids put in danger in their own backyard. I'm going to have this place crawling with people. I've already called the police and the TV stations. And now I'm going to get your job taken away. Yes," she says into the phone. "We have a problem here on Dorset." She walks toward her neighbor's house while she talks.

Dr. Mac's right eyebrow is arched high. "Gary Snyder," she says sternly, "please tell me you had that meeting with the residents, the one where you were going to explain the TVSR program to them."

Gary looks ten years old all of a sudden. His face turns red, and his eyes look everywhere except at Dr. Mac's face. In the distance, Mrs. Frazier punches another number on her cell phone and then yells into it. Gary may be a great Animal Control officer, but unfortunately, he's an absent-minded one.

"You did have the meeting, didn't you?" Dr. Mac asks.

He takes a deep breath. "Well, it's just that we had some loose dogs, and then a deer was wandering around the new development, and I've had twelve skunk calls since Saturday, and—well...it slipped my mind," he admits.

Dr. Mac closes her eyes like she's got a headache.

"What do we do now?" I ask.

"Exactly what we came here for," Gary says. "These cats are safe. They won't harm anyone. I say let's finish the job. Release the cats, trap the next batch, and then go home. I'll schedule an emergency meeting with the neighbors tonight, I promise."

"But what if Mrs. Frazier does something to hurt them?" I say.

"You can't ignore Mrs. Frazier," Dr. Mac says. "She's furious. Let's take the cats back to the clinic and keep them there a few more days. We'll release them after the meeting."

The four caged cats still in the back of the pick-up truck start to yowl. I bet they can tell they're close to home. They want to get out.

Gary kicks a pebble toward the railroad tracks. "That wouldn't be fair to the cats. They have been through a lot of stress being captured and treated. Let's release them now, then we'll set up the meeting. It will just take a minute."

Dr. Mac studies the cats, then nods once. Gary jogs back to his truck to get two more cages.

"I think Gary's right. The best thing for them right now is to set them free. There is plenty of space back here. I'll talk to Mrs. Frazier and her kids about not leaving food out for the cats. If they stop doing that, then the ferals won't stay so close to the houses. Now back to the van, everyone."

"Dr. Mac," I say, pointing to the road, "you might need to have that emergency meeting right now."

A crowd has gathered around Gary's truck. It is not a welcoming committee.

"What are you doing?" asks an angry man.

"Get rid of those filthy cats!" another man says. "I'll do it myself if you won't."

"You said you were getting rid of them," Mrs. Frazier says.

"Who's protecting the children?" asks a concerned woman.

"Who's protecting us?" asks the woman next to her.

Gary ignores what they are saying to him and carries the cages down to the clearing.

Dr. Mac walks into the middle of the crowd. "Please, if you will all just listen to me, I will explain," she says loudly. "Let's all calm down."

A police car pulls up, followed by a TV news van and another Animal Control truck. What would Mother say if she were here? She'd say this is getting out of hand.

Maggie's eyes get wide. *"Now* what's going to happen?" she asks.

"This would be a great TV show, if it weren't true," Zoe observes.

Gary's boss waves him over. I can't hear what they're saying, but it looks like a tense conversation. I think he's in trouble.

The crowd in front of Dr. Mac grows louder and louder.

"Didn't you read the article in the paper about that poor girl who got rabies?" asks one person. "That could happen to our kids, you know. We have a right to keep them safe!"

I hide my bandaged hand behind my back. No use making matters worse.

"The girl did not get rabies. She's being treated for possible exposure," Dr. Mac tells the crowd. "No one understands the risks of unvaccinated animals better than I do. We keep the cats who are being treated until we are certain they have no diseases they could pass on to people." Her voice is strong and firm.

"Maybe we should walk back to the clinic," I suggest quietly to my friends. "I don't want anyone to recognize me. If they start up with the whole rabies thing, we'll never be able to help these cats."

"And leave all this?" Brenna says. "No way!"

"No one even knows we're here," Maggie says. "Don't worry about it, Sunita."

Gary turns away from his boss and starts to load

the empty traps into the truck. He won't look at us or say anything. Mrs. Frazier hurries over to the truck to talk to him some more.

"Psst! Sunita. Over here!"

A bush is calling my name.

"Sunita!"

The bush rattles and the face of Jamie Frazier briefly appears, with Katie next to him. "Over here," he repeats. "Hurry!"

I glance at the crowd. All the grownups are busy yelling at each other, and my friends are watching them. No one else heard Jamie.

I scurry over to Jamie's hiding place. "What are you doing out here?" I ask quickly.

"We need help," Jamie whispers.

"Can't it wait?" I ask. If Mrs. Frazier sees her kids out here while Gary is releasing the ferals, she'll flip out.

Jamie shakes his head. "This is really important. That black cat you were looking for, Mittens—she's having her babies."

"Really? That's great!" I shout—then clap my hand across my mouth. I don't want to call any attention to us. "So what's the problem?" I whisper.

"She started having the kittens yesterday," Jamie says. "I think it's taking too long. She doesn't look good. Can you come look? Please."

I look back at the crowd.

The police officer is talking to Dr. Mac. The crowd seems a little calmer now, but some people are still frowning. The television crew is pointing its cameras at the crowd.

If I interrupt Dr. Mac, everyone will notice and someone might recognize me as the girl from the newspaper story.

"All right, here's what we'll do," I say. "Take me to Mittens. First, I'll see how she's doing, then you two go back inside your house and wait. Where is she?"

"Follow me!" Jamie says.

Keeping one eye on the crowd, we quickly cross the railroad tracks and dash across the clearing.

"She's under there," Jamie says, pointing under the boxcar.

I crouch down to see. Jamie and Katie kneel next to me. Mittens is under the boxcar, right at the front edge. There is one kitten on the ground near her, but it's dead. I shudder.

"Stay back, Katie," I say. I don't want her to see this. It's kind of gross and scary.

Mittens is pushing hard, trying to make the next kitten come out. She meows in pain. I can't tell what's wrong, but I know we should get her to the clinic.

"OK, listen to me," I tell Jamie. "I want you to take Katie home. There's no use getting you in trouble for this. I'm going to get Dr. Mac. Mittens needs to go to the clinic right now."

Jamie nods. "Can't you just pick her up and carry her?" he whispers.

Katie pokes me in the back. I ignore her—I'm too worried about Mittens.

"I'm afraid I might hurt her," I say. "We don't know what's going on. I've never seen a cat have kittens before."

Katie pokes again. "Su-Sunita," she says anxiously.

I turn around to find a raccoon trapping us against the boxcar. "Look out!" I cry.

The raccoon's teeth are bared, and saliva drips from its mouth. My heart starts to pound. Raccoons are nocturnal animals. They rarely come out in the day unless...they have rabies.

THIRTEEN

*M*ommy!" Katie screams.

The crowd around Gary's truck stops yelling and arguing, and turns to look across the tracks at us.

"Stay back," I tell Katie and Jamie. I grab their shirts and pull them behind me.

Mrs. Frazier starts to run toward us, but two men stop her. "Let me go!" she screams. "Jamie! Katie!"

"Everyone, stay where you are," the police officer orders, walking slowly toward the rail bed. He puts his hand on his gun. "I won't fire until I have a clear shot."

The raccoon steps closer and glares at me with poisonous yellow eyes. This is what full-blown rabies looks like. The disease has infected the raccoon's brain, and it's not afraid of anything. All it wants to do is attack—attack us!

Jamie struggles to break free.

"Don't move," I tell him.

"We have to get away!" he says in a panicked voice.

"No," I say firmly. "The raccoon is too close. If we try to run, it'll catch us. Don't move."

"We can't stay here!" Jamie says.

"I'm scared," Katie cries.

The train whistle blows in the distance. In a minute it's going to cut us off from our escape route. I have to think of something—fast.

"Shhh, it will be OK," I say, sounding more confident than I feel. I reach behind me to the open door of the boxcar and fumble around for something—anything—I can use to protect us. My fingers close around small bits of something. Gravel? Cat food! Maybe I can throw it at the raccoon, then we can run.

I slowly bring my hand around.

Underneath the boxcar, Mittens meows in pain. The raccoon's eyes dart around, then stop. He sees her lying just behind my ankles. He takes another step toward us.

Just then, the long train to Philadelphia roars past. Dust is swirling everywhere. I squint and blink my eyes. I can't see the grownups on the other side of the tracks. They can't see us, either. We're trapped! I've got to do something quick.

I throw the cat food at the raccoon. It lands behind him. Three stray cats rush out from the weeds. "Merow!" They're hungry and think we're feeding them.

The raccoon turns to look at the cats. I glance over, too. It's the gray cat with the crooked tail, one of the black-and-white strays, and—"Socrates! Where have you..."

"Fsssst!" Socrates has no time for small talk. He and the other cats stand with their backs arched, ready to defend their territory and their food. They stare down the intruding raccoon. Socrates hisses, his coat puffed out. The crooked-tail cat lowers his ears.

Just as the last train car whishes by, Socrates and the other cats leap and pounce on the raccoon, attacking with claw and tooth. The animals are a blur of fur and flashing teeth.

I swing Katie up into my arms and grab Jamie's hand, then run with them across the train tracks to safety.

"Don't shoot!" I scream at the police officer who has pulled his gun out. "Don't shoot the orange cat—he's a pet!"

The fighting animals spring apart. Socrates and

his companions flee into the weeds. The rabid raccoon snarls and bites at the air. The police officer aims his gun. I pull Katie and Jamie toward me so they won't see. I don't want to look either. I squeeze my eyes shut. Two loud shots ring out.

Oh, please, let Socrates be OK. Please.

"All clear," shouts a man. "The raccoon is dead."

By the time I look again, Dr. Mac is fighting her way into the underbrush with the rest of the Wild at Heart kids close behind her. I make sure Katie and Jamie are safe with their mother, then I join the search party. We are not going to let Socrates get away this time.

FOURTEEN

We find Socrates in the weeds beyond the boxcar. He is bleeding heavily. After wrapping him in a
towel, I carry him to the van. He's nearly uncon-
scious. Mittens isn't doing much better. Dr. Mac
says she needs an emergency cesarean to save her
kittens.

Mittens is settled into a box at my feet in the van,
and Socrates rides in my lap. His blood is soaking
through the towel and his eyes are closed.

"Stay with us, Socrates," I whisper into his torn
ear. "Just a little longer."

Dr. Mac drives to the clinic as fast as she can. I
wish she had a siren and flashing lights like ambu-
lances do for people. She parks in the driveway and
jumps out. We rush our critical patients into the
operating room. Dr. Gabe lays Socrates on the operating table while Dr. Mac wheels in a portable table

and sets Mittens on that. There's no time to waste. Both animals need surgery right away.

I've seen plenty of exams before, but not surgery. Dr. Mac gives me a serious look. "Scrub up, if you're staying," she says as she and Dr. Gabe prepare to operate. "But understand," she adds, "they might not make it."

I swallow hard and nod. "I know. But I want to help."

I wash, then slip an extra-large glove over my bandaged hand and put a rubber band around my wrist to hold the glove in place. I thought it would be cool to wear a surgical cap and gown like vets do when they operate, but I'm too worried. Dr. Gabe's scrubs are already spattered with Socrates' blood, and Mittens' heart rate is dangerously high.

"What should I do?" I ask.

Dr. Gabe doesn't even look at me. He is totally focused on trying to slow Socrates' bleeding. I really want to help Socrates, but I don't want to do anything wrong. All those cuts and blood everywhere—what if he doesn't make it?

"Over here, Sunita," Dr. Mac says.

She briskly rubs Mittens' shaved belly with a soapy sponge, then washes off the soap with alcohol and paints the skin with an iodine disinfectant.

"Hand me that package there," she says, pointing to the counter. "The one with the tube. Open it, then pass it over."

I tear the package open and Dr. Mac removes a slender, curved tube from it. She quickly opens Mittens' jaws with the fingers of her left hand and slips the tube down her throat with her right. The sedative has made Mittens completely limp. She doesn't even care that she has a tube down her throat.

"This is called a trach tube. It goes down the trachea, the windpipe, and gives me an open pathway to Mittens' lungs," Dr. Mac explains as she secures the end of the tube to Mittens' mouth with some tape. "Anesthesia machine—push it over here."

The anesthesia machine is the size of a large microwave oven on wheels, but it has a lot more dials and buttons. Dr. Mac pulls a clear plastic hose from the machine and hooks it to the trach tube.

The anesthesia puts Mittens into a very deep sleep so that she won't feel anything during the operation.

Dr. Gabe throws a piece of bloody gauze on the floor and presses a clean one onto Socrates' wound. I have never seen him look so serious.

"Surgical drapes," says Dr. Mac.

I take a bundle of pressed sheets out of a sterile package. Dr. Mac unfolds them and lays them on Mittens so that only the clipped area of her belly shows. "Almost ready now."

She attaches a little clip with a wire to Mittens' foreleg. The wire leads to a heart monitor. It measures Mittens' vital signs, how fast she's breathing, and how often her heart beats.

"See that line on the heart monitor?" Dr. Mac says. "That shows us the rhythm of Mittens' heartbeat. Her heart is beating regularly, two hundred beats a minute. That's a bit fast, but nothing to worry about. Now let's rescue some kittens."

Dr. Mac reaches for a scalpel.

"Sunita," Dr. Gabe calls. "I need your help."

I dash over to Dr. Gabe. Socrates is lying on a bloody sheet. Dr. Gabe has an I.V. bag going to keep Socrates' fluid levels up, but he really needs blood. We called the blood bank from the cell phone in the van, and they said they would send someone over right away. They should have been here by now.

Dr. Gabe frowns. "I thought I had the bleeding under control, but he must be bleeding internally as well. Call the blood bank again. Find out where that courier is."

He grabs a fresh gauze pad from a pile on the table and presses it against the open, bleeding wound on Socrates' leg. Bloody gauze litters the ground at his feet. It makes me feel kind of queasy, so I focus on the telephone, dialing quickly and asking how long until the courier arrives.

"They said it will be five more minutes," I explain as I hang up. "Is he going to make it?"

Dr. Gabe doesn't look at me. "I'm doing everything I can. More gauze. And get another I.V. bag ready, just in case."

I lay the supplies he needs at the end of the table where he can reach them. Socrates doesn't look like himself. He's lost some weight, and there are bites and cuts all over his body. He was so brave fighting that raccoon. Just thinking about it makes me want to cry. He can't die, not now. He's home. I reach out to pet his tail, but he doesn't move at all. His eyes are closed. He doesn't even know I'm here.

"That's all I need you for now," Dr. Gabe says kindly.

"How's Mittens?" I ask Dr. Mac.

"Heart rate stabilized, respiration fine. Good thing we brought her in. One of her kittens was blocking the birth canal."

"You mean she could have died?" I ask.

"Well, that won't happen now. And here is the first baby," Dr. Mac says as she lifts a tiny wet bundle out of the incision in Mittens' belly.

"Wow!" I exclaim as Dr. Mac lays the black-and-white kitten on a towel next to Mittens. "That was so fast!"

"Here's number two," Dr. Mac says as she takes out the second kitten. She snips the umbilical cord and lays the second kitten next to the first. "Grab another towel, Sunita, and clean these babies up."

"Are you sure?" I ask.

"Sure. Normally the mother cat licks the kittens clean, but since Mittens is knocked out, you'll have to do that for her."

I take the corner of a towel and gently rub the first kitten's wet fur. The kitten stretches and opens its pink mouth wide. "Look!" I cry.

"Cute, huh? Here are numbers three and four," Dr. Mac says as she sets the next pair down. "One more." She lifts the last kitten, snips the cord, and lays him with his brothers and sisters. "I think we have a new family!" she says proudly.

I glance over at Socrates. He's still limp. Dr. Gabe is frowning, still trying to stop the bleeding. Come on, Socrates, hang in there! The kittens made it—you can, too. Just a few more minutes.

The bell on the front door jangles.

"The blood's here," Dr. Mac says. "Hurry, Sunita!"

FIFTEEN

I run down the hall to the reception room. The other Wild at Heart kids are waiting there with the courier from the blood bank. Dr. Mac said only one of us could be in the operating room, and everyone decided it should be me. The courier looks surprised to see an eleven-year-old wearing surgical scrubs.

"I'll sign for it," Zoe says as she takes the clipboard from the courier's hands.

"Are they OK?" Brenna asks.

"What's going on?" Maggie asks. "How's Socrates?"

"We'll know in a few minutes," I say as I grab the small ice chest and run back to the operating room.

I thrust the ice chest into Dr. Gabe's hands. He takes a bag of dark red blood from the chest and quickly connects the tubing from it to a catheter

117

already inserted into Socrates' foreleg. In less than a minute, the blood starts flowing from the bag into Socrates.

"How do you know it's the right kind of blood?" I ask. "Aren't there a lot of different blood types?"

"Most cats have type A blood," he explains. "If Socrates were a Persian or Cornish Rex, then we'd have to type and match, because he could have type B or AB." He pauses to check the flow of the blood in the tubing. "Excellent. This will buy us some time," he says. "J.J., I could use your help."

"I'll be right there," Dr. Mac says.

Mittens has been stitched up and taken off the anesthesia, but she is still connected to the heart monitor.

"Sunita, I want you to keep an eye on Mittens' vital signs and watch the kittens closely," she tells me. "If anything looks strange, anything at all, sing out and one of us will come running." Dr. Mac peels off one pair of gloves and snaps on another, then joins Dr. Gabe to help sew up Socrates.

Socrates has to make it. With the two best vets in the world helping him, he just has to. I say a little prayer, just in case, then focus on my patients.

I never imagined anything this small could be so alive. Newborn kittens don't open their eyes for a few days, and their ears are still flat along their heads. To be honest, they don't look a whole lot like kittens, but I'm sure Mittens will think they are beautiful. I think they're beautiful.

The kittens are all snug and warm against their mother.

Suddenly, my mother bursts through the door. The vets working on Socrates look up in surprise.

"I'm sorry," Mother says. "One of my nurses heard it on the news. Was Sunita attacked by a rabid raccoon?"

"We'll let her tell you," Dr. Mac says as she turns her attention back to Socrates.

I take the sterile mask off my face. "Shh!" I say, pointing. "They're operating on Socrates. The raccoon got him, not me. I'm fine," I reassure her as she hugs me tightly.

"Is it true what they said, that you saved two small children?" She cups my chin in her hands and looks into my eyes.

"I had to," I explain. "We were trapped. But the raccoon was distracted by the cats, and I was able to get the kids to safety. Honest, I'm not hurt at all."

Mother pulls me close and hugs me so tightly I can't breathe. "I don't know what I'm going to do with you," she says.

I glance over at the heart monitor. Mittens is still doing well. "Want to see some newborns?"

The kittens make quiet mewing sounds as they huddle against their mom.

"They're so tiny!" Mother exclaims.

"They were just born a few minutes ago. I got to watch. Look, she's waking up!"

Mittens blinks her eyes, looks at each one of us, then closes her eyes. She's exhausted. Her kittens are lined up next to each other along her stomach. Their fur is fluffy now. I wish I could pick one up, but I know they need to be with their mother.

Dr. Mac walks over to join us.

"Socrates?" I ask.

"Will be fine," she assures me. "He needed two units of blood and both of us to sew him back together, but he'll be his old self in a few weeks. We boosted his rabies vaccine. I'm predicting total recovery. Knowing him, he'll be proud of the scars. How are our littlest patients?"

"Rather adorable," Mother says.

I gently pet Mittens' head. "She woke up and looked at us once, and then went back to sleep. Her heart rate stayed the same. Is she going to be OK?"

"Her babies are healthy and she's safe with us," Dr. Mac says.

My heart thumps in my chest. All the emotions of the day, of the last week, are crashing down around me. I press my lips together tightly, but I can't stop my chin from quivering. My eyes fill with tears.

"Sunita?" Dr. Mac asks. "What's wrong?"

I shake my head wordlessly, then turn to my mother. She holds me in her arms.

Now that I know everybody will survive, I can really cry.

SIXTEEN

A week and a half later, Tiger's quarantine is over. He never developed any rabies symptoms. I'm relieved for both of us—and very happy I don't need any more shots.

Brenna's parents agreed to let Tiger and a few other ferals be released into their woods. Brenna says that when Gary released Tiger, the cat dashed into the woods like he was born there. Half of the colony went to the woods, the other half back to Cat Land. That was the compromise that Gary and Dr. Mac worked out with Mrs. Frazier and her neighbors. Once they understood that the TVSR program would prevent rabies, they were willing to try it. Gary's offer to trap any other raccoons in the area helped, too.

We're gathered around the kitchen table at Dr. Mac's, finishing the vaccination reminder list.

Socrates is sitting in my lap, purring. I think he actually enjoyed his run-in with the raccoon. I wish I could get him to tell me what he was doing those days he was missing, but I guess that's a cat mystery. What matters is that he's home and healthy. And heavy!

"A little bird told me you all have another dinner date tonight," Dr. Mac says.

"Yeah," David says, "we're going to Sunita's house."

"I love Indian food," Zoe says.

"What *is* Indian food?" Brenna asks.

"It's great," I say. "But don't worry. Mother promised there would be macaroni and cheese for anyone who wanted it."

I was a little surprised when Mother agreed to let me have my friends over for dinner—and shocked when she decided to do a full Indian menu. She only does that for really important people or on holidays. She's been more interested in listening to my stories from the clinic recently, and has come in to see how our patients are doing. I never thought I would see her act this way, but I'm not complaining.

The five of us quickly finish the chores: sweeping animal hair off the floors, walking the dogs that are being boarded, and making sure all the patients in the recovery room have food and water. Just as we finish, Mother stops by to pick us up for dinner.

"Hope I'm not too early," she says.

"We're almost done," I say. "I just want to check Mittens and her family before we go."

Mother grins. When she smiles like that, she is the most beautiful woman in the world. "I'll come with you," she says.

Wow. Is this my mother?

Mittens and her kittens are resting in a roomy cage in the recovery room. Mittens looks at Mother and me and purrs like a queen receiving her visitors. Her kittens are just opening their eyes. Three of them are white, and two are tuxedos just like their mom.

I open the cage door and scratch behind Mittens' ears. She purrs louder and stretches her neck out, trying to smell Mother's hand. Mother looks nervous, but she extends her hand a few inches. Mittens bumps her head against Mother's fingertips. Mother smiles shyly.

"Well, this is one cat that doesn't scare me," Mother says.

"Cats aren't scary," I say. "I got bit because I made a mistake. Cats that are raised around people are the best pets in the world. They're smart and loving. But you have to understand and respect them."

"Giving our new family a checkup?" Dr. Mac asks as she comes into the recovery room. "Tomorrow I'm going to contact some of our regular clients to try to find someone who could temporarily take in Mittens and her brood until the kittens are old enough to leave her. It would be much better for them to be in a house than back here in recovery. They would socialize better and wind up being friendlier cats."

"No need, J.J.," my mother says. "We'll take them home with us."

"Wh-what did you say?" I can't believe what I'm hearing.

"Nothing permanent, no promises, Sunita. But if you want, we can be Mittens' foster family for a while. I recently read a report about what good pets cats make," she winks. "And you heard Dr. Mac— they need a lot of human contact. Between you and the twins, that shouldn't be a problem. Maybe I could help out, too. A little."

She struggles to stay upright as I throw myself at her and give her a big squeeze.

"Meeoww!" Mittens cries.

"You'd better see what she wants," Mother says.

125

I grin. "She doesn't want anything. She's just happy. As happy as I am!"

Feline Feelings

By J.J. MACKENZIE, D.V.M.

WILD WORLD NEWS—Some people say that cats are aloof—that they don't show their feelings and can act a little stuck-up.  Others accuse cats of being unfriendly because they don't respond to commands the way dogs do. This isn't the case at all. Your cat can tell you how she feels about you in many different ways. You just need to know how to read her signals.

READING THE SIGNS

She purrs. Purring is a mysterious sound, but it usually means your cat is cozy and content. A mother cat purrs when her babies are nursing, and cats sitting close to each other will purr in a friendly way. If your cat is in your lap and she's purring, she's telling you that she feels safe and secure.

Continued on page B5

Ocean Change Making

Continued from page B3

She kneads her front paws. Kneading, or pushing back and forth with the front paws, is another affectionate sign. Young kittens knead their mother's teats to help the milk flow. The soft, warm lap of a human may remind a cat of her kitten days, and in kneading, she is treating you like her mom. If your cat sees you as her mother, that's a compliment!

> **A WARM LAP REMINDS A CAT OF HER KITTEN DAYS.**

She greets you with a "Meow!" Not all cats are vocal, but most will greet their owners with a "Meow!" when they come home or walk into a room. It might mean "Feed me," or "I missed you!" Whatever the translation, your cat knows you are part of the family, and she's glad you are there.

She keeps her ears pointed up and facing forward. If your cat is feeling threatened or afraid, she'll flatten her ears against her head. This protects the ears from attack. If she is  feeling confident and content, her ears will be upright, swiveling every now and then to hear what is going on around her.

She bumps her head against your leg. This is called "chinning." Cats have special glands around their chins, lips, and the tops of their heads. When she rubs her head or the side of her mouth against your hand or leg, she's marking you, telling all the other cats in the world that you belong to her.

She licks you. Not all cats do this, but some will lick their owner's hand while they are being petted. If your cat does this, she may be groom-  ing you. Cats will sometimes groom other cats, or other pets they are friendly with such as a dog. This grooming is a sign of closeness.

She yawns. A yawn is a reassuring signal. If your cat yawns as you walk into a room, she's saying, "Oh, hi, there you are."

She sleeps with you. Cats are particular about their sleeping places. They need to be warm and feel very secure. If your cat sleeps with you, then she trusts that you won't hurt or startle her.

She lets you pet her. Cats are fussy about whom they will allow to pet them. If they are uncomfortable with a person, they will walk away or struggle to be put down. When your cat lets you pet her, it's a sign that she trusts you and feels good around you.✛

Dog Team
Rescues Lost Skier

COLORADO—An Ohio ~~~ ~~~pped under 2 feet of snow was rescue~~~

About the Author

Chris Whitney/Doylestown, PA

Laurie Halse Anderson has had many pets—dogs, cats, mice, even salamanders. Her first cat was named Smokey. He was a big, strong tomcat. Smokey liked to sneak into the church next door to her house, especially during weddings. One day he darted in and the heavy door closed on his tail, breaking it. His tail had to be amputated. After that, he looked so much like a bobcat that he sometimes scared people who didn't know him. But he never scared Laurie.

Laurie has written many books for kids, including picture books and a young adult novel. When she's not writing or teaching writing workshops at local schools, Laurie splits her time between bird-watching and hanging out at the local vet clinic. She lives in Ambler, Pennsylvania, with her husband, her two daughters, and a cat named Mittens.

Trickster

David
Vet Volunteer

The horse is standing in the middle of the yard, breathing hard. I can see the sweat on his chest. His eyes and ears sweep across the yard, like he's expecting something else to come along and scare him.

"Bring the water, David," Mr. Quinn says, keeping his voice nice and calm. "He's settling down nicely."

Slowly I walk down the steps. As I get to the bottom, the horse walks straight toward me.

"Don't move," Mr. Quinn tells me. If I hand the bucket to Mr. Quinn, it might startle the horse.

The horse does have a limp. It looks like it hurts him to put his full weight on his right hind foot. As he gets closer, I can see a dark red stream of blood and a cut about two inches long over his right hock.

"What's his name?" I whisper.

"Trickster," Mr. Quinn answers.

Trickster whinnies. The high-pitched sound makes the hair on the back of my neck stand up, like I just touched an electric wire. He stops in front of me, his nostrils flaring, trying to smell me.

I shift the bucket to my left arm and hold out my right hand.

"Hi, Trickster. I'm David."

Trickster stretches his neck, his eyes warm and friendly. The short hairs of his muzzle tickle as he moves his nose over my hand and up my arm to pick up my scent. I can smell him. Man, it is so good to smell a horse again! For a second, it reminds me of how Dad and I used to smell after we came home from the barn. But Dad's not here. It's just me and this magnificent horse.